The Case of the
Deadly Toy

Erle Stanley Gardner

BALLANTINE BOOKS • NEW YORK

ISBN 0-345-31272-4

This edition published by arrangement with William Morrow and Company

Printed in Canada

First Ballantine Books Edition: October 1983
Second Printing: April 1984

FOREWORD

SOME SEVEN OR EIGHT YEARS AGO I MET DR. LESTER Adelson when I attended a series of lectures given on legal medicine. He was then working under my good friend, Dr. Richard Ford, head of the Department of Legal Medicine at Harvard. Since that date I have watched Dr. Adelson's career with great interest. He is at the moment with Dr. Samuel Gerber, the coroner of Cuyahoga County in Cleveland.

I can't speak too highly of Dr. Adelson's ability, character and achievements, but he doesn't want me to speak of these. He wants me to tell something of the importance of legal medicine and what it means.

It is a mistake to believe that the forensic pathologist is always concerned with murder. It is a mistake to believe that autopsies are only for the dead. They are to help the living. There is another side to legal medicine. The courtroom side. It is a great mistake to let the highly partisan medical witness sway a jury to his way of thinking. The real scientist is never partisan.

When Dr. Adelson takes the witness stand it sometimes seems that the cross-examiner is scoring points. Actually he is doing nothing of the sort. Dr. Adelson doesn't believe that simply because a doctor is subpoenaed by the prosecution or the defense, by the plaintiff or the defendant, he owes any allegiance whatever to the side that subpoenaed him.

Dr. Adelson's creed is that an expert medical witness owes allegiance to only one master, and that is TRUTH.

As Dr. Adelson said in a letter to me, in which he discussed this problem, "Insofar as it is humanly possible, he (the medical witness) should refrain from taking sides or shading his testimony. *An answer favorable to the defense during cross-examination should be given cheerfully and promptly, without equivocation or stalling."*

Quoting again from a letter in which Dr. Adelson outlined his ideas in regard to legal medicine and its importance to the public, these thoughts of his are in my opinion highly significant:

The forensic pathologist encounters many important problems not connected with a courtroom. The notion that the forensic pathologist deals only with homicide is a too narrow and obsolete view of his multifaceted day-to-day work. The modern medico-legal investigative office, whether it be called Coroner's Office, Medical Examiner's Office, or what you will, is in reality a public health office. Although it may appear paradoxical to equate an agency that deals exclusively with the dead with public health, basically the purpose of the office is to study the dead to help the living.

Actually today's medico-legal office is a dynamic kinetic institution that can and should make a valuable and unique contribution to the community. While not for a moment minimizing the importance of homicide investigation, nonetheless murder and manslaughter account for but a small fraction (less than 4% in Cleveland) of the total case load. Accidental deaths of all types are equally deserving of study. They represent a tremendous wastage of human life. Post-mortem study frequently points the way towards measures which will prevent similar tragedies. This is true of traffic fatalities, industrial fatalities and lethal accidents in the home.

Suicide (self-murder, if you will) is twice as frequent as homicide and represents an equally untimely loss of human life. Study of these cases frequently yields data which indicate ante mortem tendencies towards self-destruction or furnish some explanation for the act, data which may give a measure of comfort to the bereaved family.

Sudden and unexpected death from natural causes may masquerade as suicide, homicide or accident and vice-versa. For many reasons it is essential that the true nature of these deaths be established. Moreover, sudden and unexpected natural death, whether it be the infant found in its crib or the previously apparently healthy adult stricken by coronary thrombosis, is a fertile field for research by the forensic pathologist in whose domain these catastrophic situations occur. Unsuspected infectious diseases, a threat to the community, may lead to sudden and unexpected death and thus present themselves to the forensic pathologist for consideration. Prompt and correct diagnosis leads to quick mobilization of prophylactic measures to prevent the development of other cases or finding them while there is still time for therapy.

Finally, the forensic pathologist has the responsibility of sharing his knowledge and experience and teaching those in a student status, undergraduate or postgraduate. The forensic autopsy table is probably the best point of departure for studying the effects of trauma, whether chemical, electrical, thermal or mechanical, on the human organism. Thoughtful observations in the post-mortem room point the way to rational treatment at the bedside.

In summary, the forensic pathologist studies those deaths where the public interest is involved. He is an impartial fact-finder in a most favorable position— he can rise above the partisan conflict. Never should he invade the province of the jury or usurp the prerogatives of the prosecutor.

I have attended a good many murder trials. I have listened to a good many expert medical witnesses. Some of them have been fair, impartial and just; some of them partisan, clever and biased.

Unfortunately it is this latter type which is in great demand. Too many lawyers like to call expert witnesses who help them win cases. The highly articulate partisan "expert" is called again and again while the conscientious really impartial expert is left to spend his time in the laboratory.

I wish that every reader who sees these lines and who is subsequently called on to do jury duty would remember the above words of Dr. Adelson.

Whenever you hear one of these experts deliberately trying to advance one side of the case, trying to impress the jury, feeding it just as much propaganda as is possible with his testimony, think back on these words of Dr. Adelson, think back on his quiet dignity, his high standards of ethics, his devotion to truth, and his absolute fairness to both sides.

The glib partisan expert may win cases for the side that calls him, but men like Dr. Adelson are the ones who are advancing the welfare of mankind and who are slowly but surely bringing about a more dignified concept of courtroom testimony.

And so, with deep respect and admiration, I dedicate this book to my friend,

LESTER ADELSON, M.D.

—ERLE STANLEY GARDNER

CAST OF CHARACTERS

1

WITH THE POLITENESS THAT CHARACTERIZED EVERYthing he did, Mervin Selkirk said to Norda Allison, "Excuse me, please."

Then he leaned forward and slapped the child's face —hard.

"Little gentlemen," he said to his seven-year-old son, "don't interrupt when people are talking."

Then Mervin Selkirk settled back in his chair, lit a cigarette, turned to Norda Allison and said, "As you were saying . . . ?"

But Norda couldn't go on. She was looking at the hurt eyes of the child, and realized suddenly that that wasn't the first time his father had slapped him like that.

Humiliated, fighting back bitter tears in order to be "a little man," the boy turned away, paused in the doorway to say, "Excuse me, please," then left the room.

"That's his mother's influence," Mervin Selkirk explained. "She believes in discipline from a theoretical standpoint, but she can't be bothered putting it into practical execution. Whenever Robert returns from visiting with her in Los Angeles, it's a job getting him back on the beam."

Suddenly in that instant Norda saw Mervin Selkirk in his true character. The indolent, smiling politeness, the affable courtesy of his manner, was a mask. Beneath the partially contemptuous, partially amused but always polite manner with which he regarded the world, was a sadistic streak, an inherent selfishness which covered itself with a veneer of extreme politeness.

Abruptly Norda was on her feet, stunned not only by

her discovery, but by the clarity with which her new realization of Mervin's character came into mental focus.

"I'm afraid I'm bushed, Mervin," she said. "I'm going to have to leave you now. I've been fighting a beastly headache, and I'm going home to see if some aspirin and a little rest won't help."

He jumped up to stand beside her. His left hand reached out and caught her wrist in a tight grip.

"Your headache was rather sudden, Norda."

"Yes."

"Is there anything I can do?"

"No."

He hesitated then, just as he had hesitated for a moment before slapping the child. She felt him gathering forces for an onslaught.

Then it came with no preliminary.

"So you can't take it."

"Can't take what?"

"Disciplining a child. You're a softie."

"I'm not a softie, but there are ways of disciplining children," she said. "Robert is sensitive; he's intelligent and he's proud. You could have waited until I had left and explained to him that it wasn't gentlemanly to interrupt, then he'd have accepted the correction.

"You didn't do that. You humiliated him in front of me. You undermined his self-respect, and—"

"That will do," Mervin Selkirk said coldly. "I don't need a lecture on parental discipline from an unmarried woman."

"I think," Norda said quietly, "I'm just beginning to really know you."

"You don't know me yet," he told her, his eyes threatening and hard. "I want you, and what I want I get. Don't think you can walk out on me. I've noticed lately that you've been talking quite a bit about that Benedict chap who works in the office with you. Perhaps you don't realize how frequently you're quoting him. It's Nate this and Nate that— Remember this, Norda,

2

you've announced your engagement to me. I won't let any woman humiliate me. You've promised to marry me and you're going through with it."

For a moment his fingers were like steel on her wrists, his eyes were deadly. And then, almost instantly, the mask came back. He said contritely, "But I shouldn't bother you with these things when you're not feeling well. Come dear, I'll take you home. . . . I'm really sorry about Robert. That is, I'm sorry if I hurt you. But, you see, I happen to know Robert quite well, and I think I know *exactly* how he should be handled."

That night, after giving the matter a lot of thought, Norda wrote a formal letter breaking her engagement to Mervin Selkirk.

Three nights later she went out with Nathan Benedict for the first time. They went to the restaurant which Nate knew was Norda's favorite. There was no incident. Two nights later Mervin called to ask if he might talk with her. "It won't do any good," she told him. "Anyway, I'm going out tonight."

"With Nate?" he asked. "I understand you let him take you to *our* restaurant."

"It's none of your business," she snapped and slammed the phone back into its cradle.

Later on when the phone rang repeatedly she didn't answer it.

Nate came for her promptly at eight.

He was tall, slender in build, with wavy, dark-brown hair and expressive eyes. They went once more to the same restaurant.

There was some delay at the table reservation. It was suggested they wait in the cocktail lounge.

Norda didn't see Mervin Selkirk until it was too late, nor could she swear afterward that he had actually thrust out his foot so that Nathan Benedict stumbled.

There were plenty of witnesses to what happened after that.

3

Mervin Selkirk got to his feet, said, "Watch who you're pushing," and hit Benedict flush on the jaw.

As Benedict went down with a broken jaw, two of Mervin's friends, who were seated at the table, jumped up to grab his arms. "Take it easy, Merv," one of them said.

There was a commotion, with waiters swarming around them, and eventually the police. Norda had been certain she had seen a glint of metal as Mervin Selkirk's right hand had flashed across in that carefully timed, perfectly executed smash.

The surgeon who wired Benedict's broken jaw was confident the injuries had been caused by brass knuckles. However, police had searched Selkirk at Norda's insistence and had found no brass knuckles; nor were there any on the friend who was with Selkirk and who volunteered to let the police search him. The second friend who had been with Selkirk had disappeared before the police came. He had had an engagement, Selkirk explained and he didn't want to be detained by a lot of formalities. He would, however, be available if anybody tried to make anything of it.

Selkirk's story was quite simple. He had been sitting with his friends. His back was to the door. Benedict, in passing, had not only stepped on his foot, but had kicked back at his shin. He had got to his feet. Benedict had doubled his fist. Mervin Selkirk admitted he had beat Benedict to the punch.

"What else was there to do?" he asked.

A week after that, Norda Allison began to get the letters. They were mailed from Los Angeles, sent air mail to San Francisco. They were in plain stamped envelopes. Each envelope contained newspaper clippings; sometimes one, sometimes two or three. All of the clippings dealt with stories of those tragedies which are so common in the press: The divorced husband who couldn't live without his wife, who had followed her as she walked from the bus and shot her on the street. The jilted suitor who had gone on a drinking spree, had then invaded the apartment where his former fiancée lived and fired five shots into her body. The drink-crazed man who had walked into the office where his former girl friend was working, had said, "I can't live without you. If I can't have you, no one else will." Desipite her screams and pleading, he had shot her through the head, then turned the gun on himself.

Norda, naturally, had seen such stories in the press, but since they hadn't concerned her, she had read them casually. Now she was startled to find how many such cases could be assembled when one diligently clipped stories from the papers of half a dozen large cities.

She went to a lawyer. The lawyer called in the postal authorities. The postal authorities went to work and the letters continued to come.

It was impossible to get any proof. The person mailing the letters evidently wore gloves. There was never so much as the smudge of a fingerprint which could be developed in iodine vapor. The envelopes were mailed in drop boxes in various parts of Los Angeles. Norda Allison's name and address had been set in type on a small but efficient printing machine, such as those frequently given children for Christmas.

At the suggestion of Norda's lawyer, Lorraine Selkirk Jennings, Mervin's divorced wife, who was now living in Los Angeles with her second husband, was consulted. She remembered having given Robert a very expensive printing press for Christmas the year before. Robert had taken it to San Francisco when he went to visit his father. It was still there. Mervin Selkirk had, it seemed, enjoyed the press even more than his son.

This information gave Norda's lawyer ground for jubilation. "Now we'll get him," he gloated. Norda made an affidavit. Her attorney handled it from there. Police served a search warrant on Mervin Selkirk.

The printing press was located without difficulty. From the condition of the rollers, it was evident it hadn't been used in some time. Moreover, the experts gave it as their opinion that the envelopes had most certainly not been addressed on that press. The type was of a different sort.

Mervin Selkirk was excessively polite to the officers. He was only too glad to let them search the place. He was surprised to find Miss Allison had been having trouble. They had been engaged. He was quite fond of her. The engagement had been broken over a minor matter. Miss Allison was working altogether too hard and had been under great nervous tension. She had not been like herself for some weeks before the engagement was broken. If there was anything Mervin could do, he wanted it understood he was willing to help at any time. He would be only too glad to render any financial assistance in tracking down the persons who were annoying Miss Allison. The police were welcome to drop in at any time. As far as he was concerned, they didn't need any search warrant. His door would always be open to the authorities. And would they please convey to Miss Allison his sincere sympathy. He admitted he had tried to call her himself a couple of times, but she had hung up as soon as she recognized his voice.

It wasn't until Lorraine Selkirk Jennings called long distance that Norda's frayed nerves began to give way.

"Was it the printing press?" she asked Norda.

"No," Norda said. "The press was there all right but it hadn't been used for some time."

"That's just like him," Lorraine said. "I know exactly how his mind works. He saw Robert's press. He then went out and got one similar to it, but with different type. He probably printed about two hundred envelopes in advance, then he took the press out on his yacht and dropped it overboard. He knew you'd suspect him; that you'd find out about Robert's press and get a search warrant—that's his way of showing you how diabolically clever he is. I'm surprised you went with him as long as you did without recognizing the sort of man he is beneath his mask."

Norda resented Lorraine's tone. "At least I found out in time to avoid marrying him."

Lorraine laughed. "You were smarter than I was," she admitted. "But you'll remember I dropped you a note telling you not to be fooled."

"I thought it was the result of jealousy," Norda said somewhat ruefully.

"Heavens, I'm happily married again," Lorraine said. "I was trying to save you from what I'd gone through with him. . . . If I could only get sole custody of Robert, I wouldn't want anything more."

Norda said apologetically, "Of course, Mervin told me stories about you. I was in love with him—or thought I was, and it was only natural for me to believe him, since I'd never met you."

"I understand," Lorraine agreed sympathetically. "Let's not underestimate either the man's cleverness or his ruthless determination, my dear. He'll stop at nothing and neither will his family.

"I tried to stick it out for Robert's sake, but I could take only so much. I left him when Robert was four and returned to Los Angeles, since it was my home.

"The family is even more powerful here than in San Francisco. They retained a battery of clever lawyers, hired detectives, and they threw mud all over me. Some of it stuck. Three witnesses perjured themselves about Robert and about me. Mervin managed to get part-time custody of Robert. He doesn't really care about Robert. He only wanted Robert so he could hurt me. I'm happily married now to a normal man, who's normally inconsiderate, who grumbles when things don't go to suit him and puts the blame on me for some of his own mistakes. I can't begin to tell you what an unspeakable relief it is.

"I'm terribly glad you broke the engagement, but don't underestimate Mervin. He simply can't stand being humiliated and he'll hound you until finally he gets you where you lose the will to resist."

7

"Will he . . . I mean, is he . . . dangerous?" Norda asked.

"Of course he's dangerous," Lorraine said. "Perhaps not in the way you think, but he's scheming, cunning, completely selfish and cruel. He had detectives shadowing every move I made. . . . Of course you're not vulnerable that way, but be careful."

Norda thanked her and hung up. She remembered the torrid charges Mervin had hurled against Lorraine at the time of the divorce. She remembered something of the testimony in the sensational trial, and Lorraine's tearful protests of innocence. At the time, Norda had not even met Mervin Selkirk and reading the newspapers she had considered Lorraine's charges of a frame-up the last ditch defense of an erring wife who had been detected in indiscretions . . . after all, where there had been so much smoke there must have been some fire.

Now Norda wasn't so certain.

It was at this time that Norda made a discovery about law enforcement.

The officers were nice about it; were, in fact, exceedingly sympathetic. But they pointed out that they had their hands full trying to apprehend persons who had broken the law. They didn't have enough men to furnish "protection" on a day-to-day basis.

To be sure, if they had definite evidence that a crime was about to be committed, they would assign men on what was technically known as a "stake-out." That was the most they could do.

They knew hardly a day passed without some jealous, estranged husband, some jilted suitor taking a gun and committing murder. The police would like to prevent those murders, but, as they pointed out, for every murder that was actually committed there were hundreds, perhaps thousands, of threats by neurotic individuals who were simply trying to "throw a scare" into the recipient of their affections and so frighten her into reconciliation.

It was, the police pointed out, something like the women who threaten to commit suicide by taking sleeping pills if their lovers don't return. Many women actually had carried out such threats and had committed suicide. Many thousands of others did not.

The police told Norda that it took evidence to convict a person of crime. It took far more than mere guesswork. There had to be evidence which was legally admissible in a court of law, and, moreover, such evidence had to prove the guilt of the accused beyond all reasonable doubt.

The police suggested that Norda Allison pay no attention to the clippings she was receiving in the mail. After all, they pointed out, the situation had existed now for some time and if Mervin Selkirk had really intended to resort to violence, he would have done so quite a bit earlier.

Norda reminded them of Nathan Benedict's broken jaw, but the police shrugged that aside. After all, the evidence in that case was in sharp conflict. Even Nathan Benedict admitted that he had "stumbled" over Selkirk's foot. He had felt that Selkirk had deliberately tripped him; but the cocktail lounge was crowded, the light was poor, Benedict had been looking towards the bar and not down on the floor, and he could only surmise what must have happened. Since Selkirk was abundantly able to respond in damages, Benedict's recourse was a civil action for violent and unprovoked assault.

It was at this point that Lorraine Selkirk Jennings again telephoned Norda Allison.

"Norda," she said excitedly, "I have news for you. I can't tell it to you over the phone. It's something we can do that I feel certain will be of a lot of help. You can help me and I can help you. Can't you possibly come down? If you could catch a plane after office hours, my husband and I could meet you, and you could get back on the first plane in the morning. Or you could come Friday, have the week end for a talk and get back without being all tired out."

Lorraine sounded full of enthusiasm, but refused to

give Norda even a hint of what she had in mind. So Norda agreed to fly down on Friday night, stay over Saturday and come back Sunday.

The next day she received two tickets in the mail, a flight down on United, a return flight on Western. There was a note from Lorraine:

My husband and I will meet the flight. Wear gloves, keep the left-hand glove on and carry your right-hand glove in your left hand. I don't drive any more. An accident I had left an indelible imprint but Barton is a wonderfully clever driver. We'll both meet you.

We got a ticket back on another airline just in case anyone should be having you followed. Please take all precautions after you leave the office. Get a cab, be certain you're not being followed, then go to one of the hotels and switch to another cab before going to the airport. We'll meet you.

Norda read the letter with amusement. She saw no reason to pay out all that money in cab fares. She confided in Nate and it was Nate who picked her up in his car an hour and a half before the plane was scheduled to leave, made a series of complicated maneuvers to be certain he was not being followed, and then drove her to the airport.

2

COMING UP THE RUNWAY AT THE LOS ANGELES AIR-
port, at ten o'clock that night, Norda Allison looked anx-
iously at the little group of people who were surveying
incoming passengers. She wore one glove on her left hand,
carrying the right-hand glove conspicuously in her left
hand.

Suddenly there was a flurry of motion and Lorraine
was hugging her.

"Oh, Norda," she said, "I'm so glad—so glad you
could make it! This is Barton Jennings, my husband—why,
you're beautiful! No wonder Mervin is crazy about you!"

Norda shook hands with Barton Jennings, a stocky,
quiet, substantial individual, and listened to Lorraine
carry on a conversational marathon while they walked to
the baggage claiming counter.

"You're going to stay with us," Lorraine said. "We
have a nice spare room and we can put you up without
any trouble. Barton is going over and get the car, then he'll
drive around to pick us up and by that time your baggage
will be ready. Let me have your baggage check, dear. I
have a porter here who knows me."

"What's it all about?" Norda asked.

"Norda, it's one of the greatest things you've ever
seen. We're going to come out on top. I have the nicest
attorney. His name is A. Dawling Crawford. Did you ever
hear of him?"

Norda shook her head, said, "I've heard of Perry Mason down here in this part of the state. I was told to get
in touch with him if—"

"Oh, Perry Mason is for murder cases," Lorraine interrupted, "but Art Crawford—that's his name, Arthur, but he always signs it A. Dawling Crawford for some reason—is an all-around lawyer. He handles criminal cases and everything else. Norda, I'm so excited! We're going to get sole custody of Robert. I'm going to want you to testify, and—"

"Want *me* to testify!" Norda exclaimed.

Lorraine, handing Norda's baggage check to a porter, said, "Why, yes, of *course,* Norda. You understand the situation and I know that you are fond of Robert."

"But wait a minute," Norda protested, "I thought from what you said over the telephone this was something that was going to benefit *me.* All I want to do is to get Mervin Selkirk out of my hair. I want to get away from him. I want him to forget me. I want to quit receiving those newspaper clippings. I certainly don't want to get involved with him again."

"But that's just the point," Lorraine explained. "Mr. Crawford tells me that if you appear in court and testify on our behalf, then it's almost certain that Mervin will make some threats against you and *then* we can go to the judge and state that those threats were made because you are a witness in the case. Then the judge will make an order restraining him. Then it will be contempt of court if he does anything further."

"Listen," Norda said patiently, "he's done everything short of attempting murder and I'm not at all satisfied but what he'll do that next. It isn't going to be much satisfaction for me to be a corpse and to know that Mervin Selkirk is held for contempt of court. I don't care how good an attorney you have, you have to have *proof* before you can do anything. And that's just what we can't get at the present time—proof."

"But we have proof," Lorraine said. "We have a witness to whom Mervin said he didn't really have any love for Robert, that he only wanted part-time custody of him to teach me a lesson."

"That's fine," Norda said coldly, "for you. It doesn't help me with *my* problem."

"But you aren't going to let me down," Lorraine wailed.

"I don't know," Norda said, "but I do know I'm not going to get mixed up in any of Mervin Selkirk's affairs until I know exactly where I stand. I'm going to see an attorney of my own."

"This is Friday night," Lorraine said. "You can't see anyone over the week end. Mr. Crawford has made arrangements to be at his office tomorrow shortly before noon so he can take your affidavit."

Norda stood by the incoming baggage platform, thoughtfully silent.

"You aren't going to let us down. You can't," Lorraine went on. "It isn't only for me, it's for Robert. You've seen him. You know what this means to Robert. You're anxious to get away from the Selkirk family, but think of poor Robert.

"I've been trying for the last two years to get Robert's exclusive custody. Every time the matter comes up, Mervin goes into court and blandly testifies to absolute falsehoods. I am cast in the role of a woman who is trying to strike at my former husband, and Mervin is poised, suave and quite sure of himself. The last time this thing came up I told of how frightened Robert was of his father and Mervin gravely told the judge that I was solely responsible for Robert's attitude, that I had carefully and deliberately poisoned Robert's mind. Then Mervin produced witnesses who swore Mervin was the personification of fatherly love when Robert was with him.

"The judge was impressed. He made an order that Robert was to spend two months out of every year with Mervin and that I was to be particularly careful not to discuss Mervin with the boy. Then the judge continued the case for seven months.

"The seven months are up a week from Monday. Now, with this new testimony, and with your testimony, we can show Mervin up for just the sort of a man he really is. Then I can get the sole custody of Robert, and—"

"I'm not so sure you can," Norda interrupted. "Remember I only saw him slap Robert's face once."

"But you *saw* it!" Lorraine insisted. "You saw the way he did it; the hardness of the slap. You saw him reach out in that deadly, self-contained way of his and slap a little child half across the room."

"It wasn't half across the room."

'Well, it was a hard slap."

"Yes," Norda conceded, "it was a hard slap."

"Administered in front of company and only because he had interrupted you with some childish request."

Norda remained dubious, feeling somehow that she had been tricked. "After all, Lorraine, I was almost one of the family. Robert called me 'Aunt Norda' and he couldn't have been expected to be as formally polite with me as with a stranger."

"Of course," Lorraine agreed. "That's what makes the cruelty of it all the more flagrant."

Norda turned to Barton Jennings, but he forestalled the question. "Don't look at me," he laughed. "I'm just the guy who drives the car. Lorraine's troubles with her former spouse are out of bounds for me. If he comes around me, I'll bounce a hammer off his head. I don't want any part of him, but I'm trying desperately to keep out of Lorraine's private affairs. I'll furnish whatever financial help is needed. . . . Of course, I'm crazy about Robert."

"Who isn't?" Norda laughed. "By the way, where is he? I had hoped you'd bring him."

"He's leaving early in the morning for a four-day camping trip," Lorraine explained. "It's a great event for him because he can sleep out and take his dog with him. Frankly, we didn't tell him you were coming. You have no idea how much he cares for you. If he'd known you were coming, I know he'd have preferred to stay and visit with you . . . and then there would have been speculation as to why you were here and all that.

14

"We don't want Robert to know anything about all this. We think it's better that way. There'll be time for a visit with you on some more propitious occasion. You must come and spend a week with us after all of this is ironed out."

Norda was silent, thinking of Robert, knowing how fond he was of her, wondering what would have happened if she hadn't broken the engagement but had gone ahead and married Robert's father. . . . Then it suddenly dawned on her that had she done so, Mervin would undoubtedly have used her affection for Robert and the child's regard for her as a lever to get at least half-time custody of Robert.

With a sudden shock she wondered if Lorraine had ever considered this possibility.

As soon as she had that thought, she felt certain Lorraine had at least explored the possibilities. It wouldn't be like her not to have thought of that. Any woman would have. And Mervin had admitted a reluctant admiration for Lorraine's foresight and mental agility. "There's one thing about my former wife," he had told Norda, "she never overlooks a bet. She is constantly chattering and has a babyface, but she's as cold-bloodedly accurate as an adding machine and she lies awake nights thinking of the things that will happen if such and such takes place."

Norda's thoughts were interrupted by Lorraine, who had been studying her face. "At least, Norda, you'll come out to spend the night with us and then talk with our lawyer tomorrow morning. I know you'll see things in a different way after that."

At that point Norda would have much preferred to have gone to a hotel, but Lorraine was so insistent that she permitted herself to be driven to the Jennings' home in Beverly Hills.

She asked where Robert was sleeping and was told he was in a tent in the patio. Of late he had become quite an out-of-door character, watching television shows featuring the famous plainsmen of the west. He had finally insisted on moving from his bedroom and sleeping outside.

Lorraine said they usually had a baby sitter for him when they were out. Tonight, however, both of their favorite baby sitters were tied up and couldn't come. So they had waited until Robert was asleep in his tent in the patio, and then had driven to the airport.

They had known he would be quite safe because Rover would be on guard. Rover was the Great Dane Lorraine had insisted on keeping when she had made her property settlement with Mervin. Norda had heard Robert talk about the dog, and then she herself had been "introduced" to the animal once when Robert was visiting Mervin.

The dog was a huge creature with great dignity and expressive eyes. He had taken to Norda and to her delight had remembered her when he had next seen her, waving his tail and showing his pleasure when she stroked his forehead.

Barton Jennings went to the back door to look out in the patio. He reported everything was all right, that Rover was asleep where he could keep one eye on the house, one on Robert's tent.

Norda asked about going out to speak to the dog, but Barton said he'd probably get excited, make a noise and waken Robert.

Once Robert knew Norda was there, Lorraine said, he'd be certain to refuse to go on the camping trip and that wouldn't be fair to the other boys, or to Robert himself.

There was something in her voice that gave Norda a vague sense of disquiet. Robert and Norda had been great pals. She felt she had won Robert's complete confidence. Was it possible there was an element of jealousy on the part of Lorraine?

She dismissed the thought as soon as it occurred to her,

pleaded fatigue from a long day, and was shown to her bedroom, a second-floor front room on the northwest side of the house.

3

PERRY MASON LATCHKEYED THE DOOR OF HIS PRIVATE office to find his secretary, Della Street, waiting for him.

Mason made a little grimace of distaste. "Saturday morning," he said, "and I have to drag you out to work."

"The price of success," Della Street told him smilingly.

"Well, you're good-natured about it, anyway."

Della Street made a sweeping gesture, which included the office, the desk with its pile of correspondence, the open law books which Mason was to use in the brief he was about to dictate. "It's my life and it's yours. We may as well face it."

"But it's work," Mason said, watching her face. "There are times when it must be sheer drudgery for you."

"It's more fascinating than any type of play," she said. "Are you ready?"

She opened her notebook and held a pen poised over the page.

Mason sighed and settled into his chair.

The private unlisted telephone rang.

There were only three people in the world who had the number of that telephone. Perry Mason himself, Della Street, his confidential secretary, and Paul Drake, head of the Drake Detective Agency, which had offices on the same floor with Perry Mason.

"How does Paul know we're here?" Mason asked.

"He saw me coming up in the elevator," Della Street said. "He told me he had something he might bother us with. I warned him that you wouldn't interrupt dictation this morning for anything short of murder."

Mason picked up the telephone. "Hello, Paul. What's the trouble?"

Drake's voice came over the wire. "Despite the fact Della told me you are working on an important brief this morning and don't want to be disturbed, Perry, I thought I should call you. There's a young woman in my office who insists she *must* see you. She's really worked up, almost hysterical, and . . ."

Mason frowned. "I can't see anyone this morning, Paul. Perhaps this afternoon . . . how did she happen to come to you?"

"The telephone directory," Drake explained. "Your office number is listed for daytime calls and then my number is given for night calls and on Saturdays. She called the office and sounded so worked up that I decided I'd talk with her. I hadn't intended to pass her on to you, but I think you may want to talk with her, Perry."

"What's her name?"

"Norda Allison."

"What's it about?"

"It's quite a story. You'll like her. She's good-looking, clean-cut, fresh and unspoiled. And this trouble of hers has engulfed her. She feels she should go to the police, she thinks she's probably in danger, and yet she doesn't know just what to do."

Mason hesitated a moment, then said, "All right, Paul, send her down. Tell her to knock on the door of the private office and I'll let her in."

"A young woman, I take it," Della Street said. "I gather Paul Drake told you she was very good-looking."

Mason raised his eyebrows in surprise. "How did you know that? Could you hear what he said?"

Della Street laughed. "You impressionable men! She's sold Paul Drake and now she's selling you."

"It'll only be a short time," Mason promised. "We'll give her fifteen or twenty minutes to tell her story, and then we'll get on with the brief."

Della Street smiled knowingly, made it a point to close her shorthand notebook, put the cap back on her pen.

"I see," she said demurely.

A timid knock sounded at the door of Mason's private office.

Della Street crossed over and opened the door.

"Good morning," she said to Norda Allison. "I'm Della Street, Mr. Mason's secretary, and this is Mr. Mason. What's your name, please?"

Norda Allison stood in the doorway, seemingly in something of a daze. "I'm Norda Allison," she said, "from San Francisco. I . . . oh, I'm so sorry to bother you this morning. Mr. Drake told me you were working behind closed doors on a most important matter, but . . . well, I'd always heard that if anyone got into trouble—that is, real serious trouble, Mr. Mason was the man to see, and . . ."

Her voice trailed away into silence.

Della Street, giving the visitor the benefit of a swift and professional appraisal, indicated her approval. "Come in, Miss Allison. Mr. Mason is very busy, but if you can tell your story just as succinctly as possible, perhaps he can help you. Please try and be brief."

"But give us *all* the facts," Mason warned.

Norda Allison seated herself, said, "Are you acquainted with the Selkirk family?"

"*The* Selkirks?" Mason asked. "Horace Livermore Selkirk?"

She nodded.

"He owns about half the city down here," Mason said dryly. "What about him?"

"I was engaged to his son, Mervin."

Mason frowned. "Mervin is in San Francisco, isn't he?"

She nodded. "I'm from San Francisco."

"All right, go ahead," Mason said, "tell us what happened."

She said, "Mervin has been married before. His wife, Lorraine, is now married to Barton Jennings. There was one child of the first marriage, Robert. I am very fond of him and I was, of course, fond of Mervin."

Mason nodded.

Swiftly, Norda told Mason of her experiences with Mervin Selkirk, of her trip to Los Angeles, of spending the night at the Jennings' house.

"I take it something happened at the house last night that upset you?" Mason asked.

She nodded. "I was nervous. I went to bed and took a sleeping pill. The doctor told me this campaign of sending me newspaper clippings was doing me more harm than I realized. He gave me some quieting pills to take at night when I felt on edge.

"Last night, after I found out what Lorraine really wanted, I was terribly upset. When that first pill didn't quiet my nerves, I got up and took another. That really did the trick."

Mason watched her shrewdly. "Something happened during the night?" he asked.

She nodded. "It was this morning. However, I did think I heard—a shot in the night."

"A shot?" Mason asked.

She nodded. "At least I thought it was a shot. I started to get up, and then I heard a boy crying. I guess that must have been Robert, but that second sleeping pill really laid me out. I kept thinking I *should* get up, but put off doing so, and then I guess I just went back to sleep."

"All right," Mason said. "What happened when you finally wakened?"

"It was this morning, really early—I guess it must have been before six o'clock. I got up and there was no one around the house. I dressed and walked downstairs and opened the front door. I walked back to the patio. Robert's tent was there, the flaps of the tent were open. There was a camp cot inside with a sleeping bag, but the tent was empty. Robert had left for his camping trip. The dog went with him."

"What happened?" Mason asked. "Please tell me what upset you."

"I saw an envelope on the grass under the cot in the tent," she said. "It was an envelope exactly the same as the ones I had been receiving. My name was printed on it. Robert had started a letter to me."

She opened her purse, handed Mason a sheet of paper which had words penciled on it in a childish scrawl:

Dear Aunt Norda:
   I found this inveloape in the basment. It has your name on it. I will rite you and put it in. I want you to come see me. I am going to camp with Rover. I have a gun. We are all well. I love you.

Robert

Mason's eyes narrowed. "Go on. What did you do after you found this envelope?"

Her lips tightened. "The stamp was uncanceled. My name and address were printed on it. It was exactly the same as the envelopes I had been receiving. Robert's letter said he had found it in the basement. I tiptoed to the back door. There was a flight of stairs from the porch leading down to a rumpus room. Back of the rumpus room was a storeroom . . . well, it was there I found it."

"Found what?"

"The printing press."

"Do you mean the printing press that had been used to print the envelopes that you had been receiving in the mail?"

She nodded. "My name and my San Francisco address were still set in type on the press. The press was really a good grade of printing press, not just a toy. It had a round steel plate on top and there was printer's ink on this plate. Every time the handle was depressed, the rubber rollers would move over this inked table and the table would make a part of a revolution. Then the rollers would go down over the type and back out of the way, and the envelope or paper would be pushed up against the type."

"You examined the press?" Mason asked.

"Of course I looked at it. As I said, I'd been trying to find a printing press of that sort. After I'd complained to the postal authorities and . . . and it turned out Robert's mother had given the child a press of that sort to play with and it was still in San Francisco. . . . Of course, I went ahead and made the natural assumption that the envelopes had been printed on that press. That's typical of the way Mervin loves to play with people."

"Go on," Mason said. "Tell me about the press you found this morning."

"Well, this press had been freshly used. The ink was still sticky on it."

"How do you know?"

She looked at the tip of her middle finger. "I touched it and fresh ink came off on my finger."

"Then what?" Mason asked.

"Then," she said, "I looked a little further and there was a box with a lot of freshly printed envelopes, the same kind of stamped envelopes that had been used in forwarding those threatening clippings to me. Don't you see? It's Lorraine Jennings who is back of all this. She has been trying to poison my mind against Mervin so I would cooperate in giving testimony when she tried to get full custody of Robert."

"Now wait a minute," Mason said. "You're all mixed up. First you're talking about Mervin's diabolical ingenuity in having a printing press that would throw the authorities off the trail, and now you're making it appear that the whole thing was Lorraine Jennings' idea."

Norda thought that over for a moment, then said, "I guess I am confused, but . . . but whether I'm confused or not, I'm right. Now I suppose you'll say that sounds just like a woman—I don't care if you do—there are *other* things."

"All right," Mason said. "What are they?"

She said, "I know that a shot was fired during the night. I heard it."

"You might have heard a truck backfire."

"I heard a shot," she said, "and after that there was a sound of a boy crying. It must have been Robert. A woman was trying to comfort him. When I . . . well, when I went to the tent and looked around, I found an empty cartridge case, the kind that is ejected from a .22 automatic, lying there on the grass."

"What did you do with it?"

"I picked it up."

"Where is it now?"

"I have it here."

She opened her purse, took out the empty .22 cartridge case and handed it to Mason.

The lawyer looked it over, smelled it, then placed the empty cartridge case upright on the desk. "Did you take anything else?" he asked.

"Yes."

"What?"

"Some of the envelopes that had been printed with my name on them. I took two of them out of the box."

She took two folded stamped envelopes from her purse and handed them to Mason.

Mason studied the printed address. "Well," he said, "that's your name printed on there, and the address I assume is accurate?"

She nodded.

"And you think those are the same envelopes that . . ."

"I'm sure of it, Mr. Mason. I have here one of the envelopes which came through the mail with one of the newspaper clippings."

She handed him another envelope.

Mason compared the envelopes for a moment, then shook out the newspaper clipping which had been contained in the envelope. It had headlines, JILTED SUITOR KILLS WOMAN.

The clipping had a New York dateline and told of a jilted suitor who had waited until his ex-fiancée, who had become engaged to another man, had left the place where she was working. It was the lunch hour. He had accosted the woman on a crowded sidewalk. Frightened, the woman had turned to flee. The man had drawn a revolver, fired four shots into her, then as she lay dying on the sidewalk in front of a crowd of horror-stricken spectators, he had turned the gun on himself and blown his brains out.

Mason took a magnifying glass and compared the printing on the envelope that had been mailed, with the printing on the stamped, addressed envelope that Norda Allison had handed him.

"They seem to be the same, all right," Mason said thoughtfully. "What did you do after you made this discovery, Miss Allison?"

She said, "I suppose I was a coward. I should have gone in and confronted them with the evidence but I was so disgusted at their double-crossing and . . . and I was a little frightened . . . I guess in a way I lost my head."

"What did you *do?*"

"I didn't go through the house. I walked back out into the patio, around through the gate, into the front door which I had left unlocked, tiptoed up to the room where I had been sleeping, packed my suitcase and came downstairs. There was a telephone in the hall and I called a taxicab."

"You didn't encounter anyone in the house?"

"No one. I think they were all sleeping."

"What did you do after you took the taxicab?"

"I went to the Millbrae Hotel, registered, got a room, had breakfast and—well, at first I intended just to catch the first plane back to San Francisco. Then I kept thinking that . . . I can't explain the apprehension that I have, Mr. Mason, the feeling that something is impending that . . . I think they're intending to say I . . . I did something . . . I have that feeling."

"All right," Mason said. "There may or may not be any reason for it but there's only one thing for you to do."

"What's that?" she asked.

"Strike first," Mason told her. "When you're worried and apprehensive, assume the offensive. No one knows that you found this printing press or the envelopes?"

She shook her head. "I'm certain they don't. They were either asleep or else they had both gone with Robert to start him on his trip. There were no noises at all in the house. They told me to sleep as late as I could, that they'd call me in time to go see the lawyer."

Mason thought the situation over.

"Well, anyway there's the printing press and the stamped, addressed envelopes," he said. "That's one clue we can accept as a tangible fact—that is, if you're being completely truthful with me."

"I am. What are you going to do?"

"Call the postal inspectors. In the meantime we'll see that nothing happens to that printing press," Mason said. *"Then* we're going to let Lorraine Jennings explain how those threatening letters came to you in the mail."

"I thought that's what I should do," she said. "But it seemed so . . . so abrupt. I thought perhaps I should ask them for an explanation. I thought perhaps you could call them and—"

"And by that time the evidence would be destroyed," Mason said. "No, we'll go out there and pick up that evidence right now, and *then* Mrs. Jennings can explain how she happened to be sending you those letters."

"Do I have to go along to show the officers where it is?"

"You have to go," Mason told her, "and I'm going with you. We'll get there before the officers."

Suddenly her eyes filled with tears. "Oh, thank you, thank you!" she exclaimed. "Thank you so much, Mr. Mason, you're . . . you're wonderful."

4

MASON EASED HIS CAR TO A STOP IN FRONT OF THE house Norda indicated.

"Well," Mason said, "they're undoubtedly up by now. I saw someone moving by the window."

He opened the car door, went around and assisted Norda Allison and Della Street from the car. The trio walked up the wide cement walk to the porch and Mason rang the bell.

Lorraine Jennings opened the door.

"Well, for heaven's sake!" she exclaimed. "What in the world *happened* to you, Norda? We thought you were sleeping and didn't want to disturb you, and then finally I went up to your room and tapped gently on the door. When there was no answer, I eased the door open and you were gone. What's more, your suitcase, your personal things . . . what in the *world* happened? And . . . who are these people?"

"Permit me," Mason said. "My name is Perry Mason. I'm an attorney at law. This is Miss Della Street, my confidential secretary."

Lorraine Jennings' jaw fell open. For a moment she was speechless. Then she called over her shoulder, "Barton!"

A man's voice answered, "What is it, dear?"

"Come here," she said, "quick . . . no, no, not quick! I forgot about your arthritis."

She turned quickly to Norda. "Barton's arthritis bothered him again last night. It's his knee and when the weather's going to change it stiffens up. He's walking with a cane this morning, and . . ."

They heard the sound of the cane, of steps, and Barton Jennings stood in the doorway.

"Barton," she said, "Norda has shown up with Perry Mason, the attorney, and this is Miss Della Street, his secretary."

Barton's face showed a flash of surprise, then he bowed gravely to Della Street, shook hands with Perry Mason, said, "Well, Lorraine, what's holding us up? Invite them in. Have you folks had breakfast?"

Lorraine hesitated, then stood to one side. "Yes," she said, "do come in. What about breakfast, Norda?"

"I've had breakfast," Norda said shortly.

"And so have we," Mason said. "I want to talk to you about a rather serious matter. I am at the moment representing Miss Allison, and something happened early this morning which disturbed her greatly. I would like to discuss it, but I want you to understand that I am an attorney and that I'm representing Miss Allison. If you care to have any attorney of your own here, I would suggest you get in touch with him, or you can refer me to your attorney. But there are certain things which should be explained."

"Well, for heaven's sake!" Lorraine Jennings said. "I never heard of any such thing in my life! What in the world *are* you talking about? Norda, what *is* this?"

Norda said, "It's something I found, Lorraine. It proves exactly what you were trying to do . . . what—"

"Just a minute," Mason said. "Let me handle this, if you will, please, Miss Allison. And I suggest we all go inside."

"Well, *I'd* certainly like to know what happened," Lorraine said, leading the way into a living room. "I knew Norda was a little worried about seeing my lawyer, but there was no reason for her getting a lawyer of her own. If she didn't want to co-operate with me, all she had to do was to say so. But since she has you here, Mr. Mason, I can explain exactly what I plan to do.

"Please do sit down and let's try and get this situation

unscrambled. I've never been so absolutely bewildered in my life. I went up to Norda's room and found she'd left. . . . As I told you, Barton's bad knee started bothering him in the night and he took codeine. And I took some too because by that time he had me wide awake, what with his twisting and turning, putting on hot compresses. I didn't even hear him when he got up to take Robert and the dog out to the place where the boys were to meet at five o'clock this morning, and . . . well, I guess we owe you an apology, Norda. After Barton returned we slept pretty late. We're usually up and have breakfast a lot earlier. What in the world possessed you to leave, and *when* did you leave? If you were hungry, why didn't you just go out in the kitchen and look in the icebox? We had fruit juice, eggs—"

"Never mind that," Norda said. "Something happened which upset me."

"I think," Barton Jennings said to Mason, *"you'd* better start talking, Mr. Mason."

"Would you care to be represented by counsel?" Mason asked.

"Heavens no!" Jennings said impatiently. "We've tried to accommodate Norda Allison. My wife wanted to do her a favor. We know something of what she's been going through—that is, at least Lorraine does. Now, if you have anything to say, please go ahead and say it."

Mason said, "Did you know Miss Allison had been getting offensive matter in stamped envelopes which had been addressed by a small, hand printing press? The letters containing clippings of—"

"Of course, we did," Lorraine interrupted. "That's one of the reasons I had Norda come down here. Mervin Selkirk was bombarding her with those clippings, trying to frighten her—the poor child, I know exactly what she went through. Mervin can be the most—"

Barton Jennings interrupted his wife to say, "Just a moment, Lorraine. Let's let Mr. Mason tell us what *he* has in his mind."

Mason said, "I believe you know Miss Allison's address on those envelopes had been printed on a small hand press, Mrs. Jennings?"

"Of course I did. I'm the one who suggested to Norda that she check on a small printing press I had given my son, Robert. As I understand it, the postal authorities got hold of that press and checked it, but the envelopes couldn't have been printed on that press—the type wasn't the same."

Mason nodded gravely and said, "Miss Allison was restless this morning. She got up early, walked out in the patio and then went into a rumpus room. There's a storage room down below. She took the stairs down to the storage room."

"The old basement," Lorraine interposed.

"I suppose I had no right to," Norda apologized. "However, something happened which led me to think . . . I mean . . ."

"Norda, *please*," Lorraine interrupted. "You're our house guest. I don't suppose it's particularly usual for a house guest to get up early in the morning and go exploring, but you were our guest and I told you to make yourself at home. If you wanted to look around, it was *quite* all right. What in the world are you leading up to?"

"Simply," Mason said, "that in the basement Miss Allison found the printing press on which she believes those envelopes had been printed. She found some of the envelopes with the address on them, and her name and address were all set up in type in the printing press. Moreover, the press showed evidence of having been recently used. There was, I believe, printer's ink glistening on the steel table over which the rollers operate."

Barton Jennings motioned his wife to silence. "Just a minute, Mr. Mason. You say that Norda claims she found that in *this* house?"

Mason nodded.

"Well," Barton said, "that's very easily solved. First,

we'll go take a look at that printing press and then we'll try and determine where it came from."

"I want to warn you," Mason said, "that that printing press is evidence. I suggest that no one touch it. Miss Allison will show you where it is, but as soon as we have done that, I intend to call the authorities."

"*You* intend to?" Barton Jennings said. "What about us? We want to get at the bottom of this thing just as much as you do."

Lorraine Jennings arose, looked at Norda, and for the first time there was angry exasperation on her face. "Norda," she said, "if you found anything, why didn't you come to us? Are you absolutely certain you found what you said you did?"

"Of course I am!" Norda snapped. "I found a whole package of envelopes waiting to be used. I know now where those clippings came from. You pretended to—"

"Just a moment, just a moment," Mason interrupted. "I think Mr. Jennings and I understand the situation. It's going to be advisable for all of us to withhold comments until after we've appraised the evidence and called the officers. Now let's go take a look at that press. Will you lead the way, Miss Allison?"

"I suppose there's a shorter way," Norda said. "I went around the back, and . . ."

"Just go right through the kitchen," Lorraine said.

"Follow me," Barton Jennings said, stepping quickly forward, then grimacing with pain. "I guess you'd better do the honors, Lorraine. I forgot about the knee for the moment."

"This way," Lorraine said, and stalked across the living room, through the dining room. She flung open the door of the kitchen, crossed it and stood on the stairs leading to the rumpus room.

"Now where, Norda?" she asked.

"Down the stairs," Norda said, "then into the basement storeroom. It's just under the big shelf to the left of the stairs."

"It's going to be a little crowded for all of us to get down there," Jennings pointed out. "Why don't you and Mr. Mason go down, Lorraine? Norda can stand at the head of the stairs and direct you."

"Very well," Lorraine said, gathering up her skirt and wrapping it around her legs so it wouldn't drag on the stairs. She descended to the basement storage room. "Now where, Norda?" she called over her shoulder.

"Right to the left of a big box. You can see the handle of the printing press," Norda said.

"I don't see any handle of any printing press," Lorraine Jennings retorted.

Mason said, "Just a moment, please."

He moved over around Lorraine Jennings and peered under the shelf. "Is it behind these boxes, Miss Allison?" he asked.

"It's just back under a shelf and behind. . . . Here, I'll come down and show you."

Norda ran quickly down the stairs, pushed Lorraine to one side, held her skirt, stooped, then paused open-mouthed. "But it's no longer here!" she exclaimed.

"Let's move these boxes," Mason said. "You said that there was a box containing a package of envelopes?"

"Stamped envelopes that had been addressed and were all ready for mailing to me," Norda said.

Lorraine whipped her skirt into her lap, bent down and started pulling out boxes. "Well," she said, "here's some old recipes. I've been intending to put them into a scrapbook. Here's some letters from Mother. I suppose they might as well be thrown away. Here's . . . for heaven's sake, Barton, here's a whole box of those reprint books. I thought you were going to give them to the hospital."

"I was," Barton said from the head of the stairs, "but I hadn't finished reading them. Let's not bother with that now, Lorraine. Get the boxes cleaned out and let's see what's under the shelf."

"But," Norda protested, "there's no need to start moving everything out. It was there and now it's gone."

"*Well!*" Lorraine exclaimed, getting to her feet and shaking out her skirt. Her tone showed extreme skepticism.

"I suggest you look around, Lorraine," Barton Jennings said, "and I'd like to have Mr. Mason look around. Let's be absolutely certain that there's no foundation for this charge before we have any further discussion."

Mason prowled around through the basement storage room, moving boxes.

"Well," he said, "it would certainly appear the press is no longer in the exact place where Miss Allison saw it, at any rate."

"*No longer,*" Lorraine repeated after him furiously. "I never heard such a story in my life! I—"

"Just a moment, dear," Barton Jennings cautioned from the top of the stairs. "Let's all go back to the library and sit down."

Lorraine said coldly, "I'm afraid, Norda, that you've probably been influenced by some bad dream, to put the most courteous interpretation on it. Perhaps you took too many drugs. You said you'd been having to take pills to get to sleep."

"Well, I like that!" Norda exclaimed. "You found out that I'd been down in that basement storeroom this morning and found that printing press. So you've been very clever in getting rid of it. I suppose you've been smart enough so it can never be traced."

"I think," Barton Jennings said, "that it's going to be a lot better for all concerned if neither party makes any accusations. What do you think, Mr. Mason?"

"I think you're right," Mason said, noticing Della Street seated at a table in the rumpus room, her pen flying over the page of her shorthand notebook as she took down the conversation. "Let's go into the living room and see if we can discuss this matter quietly and intelligently."

"As far as I'm concerned, there's nothing to discuss," Lorraine Jennings said. "We invited Norda Allison to be our house guest. We tried to help her. As nearly as I can see, she has abused our hospitality. She told me she was going to take sleeping pills last night. I presume she had some drug-induced nightmare, and now she's trying to hold *us* responsible—"

"I didn't dream up those two envelopes I took out of the box," Norda Allison flared, "and which are now in Perry Mason's office." She started to mention the note she had received from Robert but then decided to leave Robert out of it. Regardless of what it might cost her, she had a feeling it might be better in the long run if neither Robert's mother nor Barton Jennings knew that it had been Robert who had first made the discovery.

"Now just a minute," Mason said. "Let's keep our heads, please. We are faced with a peculiar situation. Let me ask you, Mr. and Mrs. Jennings, do you have any objection to calling in the authorities for an investigation?"

"I certainly do!" Lorraine said. "Not until we have some tangible evidence to go on, I'm not calling in anyone. If your client wants to proceed with this absurd charge against us, Mr. Mason—well, you're a lawyer and you can tell her what the consequences will be."

Mason smiled. "I can appreciate your position, Mrs. Jennings, but under the circumstances my client is not going to be frightened. She isn't making any accusations against *you*. She is simply stating that she found an important piece of evidence in your house this morning, and, as it happens, she had the foresight to take two of the envelopes with her. I am going to have an expert examine those envelopes to see if they are the same as the envelopes she has been getting through the mail. If they are, we are going to report the entire matter to the postal authorities."

Barton Jennings said, "I think that's the wise thing to do, Mr. Mason. I can assure you that this is all news to us."

"It isn't news at all!" Lorraine flared. "She's been sending herself those notices, Barton, and now, for some reason that happens to be her personal and selfish interests, she's taken advantage of our hospitality. She brought two of those envelopes down here with her in her purse, got up this morning before anyone was up, sneaked out, went to a lawyer with those envelopes, and—"

"I repeat," Barton Jennings interrupted, "that neither party should make any accusations at this time. If it's all right with you, Mr. Mason, we'll disregard any statements and accusations which have been made by your client on the ground that she is naturally somewhat nervous and upset. And it will be agreed that your client will disregard any statements made by my wife, who is also quite naturally nervous and upset."

"I think that is probably the best way of disposing of the entire matter at this time," Mason said. "We now offer to make such an agreement with you."

"We accept that offer," Barton Jennings said.

"And now," Lorraine Jennings said to Norda, "if you'll kindly leave my house, Miss Allison, we will chalk off our attempt to befriend you as another unfortunate experience in misjudging human nature."

Mason turned to Norda Allison. "Come on, Miss Allison," he said, "let's go."

5

INSPECTOR HARDLEY CHESTER LISTENED CAREFULLY TO Norda Allison's recital of facts, then turned to Perry Mason.

"There's nothing out there now?" he asked.

"No sign of the printing press, no sign of the envelopes," Mason said.

Inspector Chester ran his hand up over the top of his head, down the back of his ears and stroked the back of his neck with his finger tips. "We can't very well go out there and accuse anyone of anything on the strength of evidence like that, Mr. Mason."

"I don't expect you to," Mason said.

"What do you expect me to do?"

"I expect you to do your duty," Mason told him.

Inspector Chester raised his eyebrows. "It's been a while since I've heard that one."

"You're hearing it now."

"What's my duty?"

"I don't know what it is," Mason said. "I'm not telling you what it is. My client made a discovery. She discovered some evidence in a case that has been bothering the postal authorities. I told her it was her duty to report what she had found. She's reported it."

"Thereby putting me in something of a spot," Chester said.

"That," Mason told him, "is something we can't control. We've told you what we found. We had a duty to do that. That duty has now been discharged."

Inspector Chester turned to Norda Allison. "You are quite certain this was a printing press?"

"Of course it was a printing press."

"You saw it plainly?"

"I saw it, I felt it, I touched it."

"And you think it had been used?"

"Of course it had been used."

"Recently?"

"It had been used for printing my name and address on those envelopes. If you don't believe me, how do you account for the fact that I have two of the stamped envelopes which bear uncanceled stamps with my name and address printed on them and that they're identical with the envelopes which were sent me through the mail?"

"I'm not saying I don't believe you. I'm asking questions. Do you have any evidence which would indicate the press had been used recently?"

"The ink was still moist on it. That is, still sticky."

"How do you know?"

"I touched the tip of my finger to it and then pulled the finger away. The ink was sticky and my finger tip was black."

"How did you clean it?"

"I opened my purse, took some cleansing tissue from a little package I carried and scrubbed my finger off."

"What did you do with the tissue?"

"It's still in the purse, I guess. I didn't want to just throw it down on the floor. I *must* have put it back in my purse, intending to throw it away as soon as I had an opportunity."

She opened her purse, fumbled around inside, then triumphantly produced a crumpled piece of cleansing tissue. There were black smears on the paper and Inspector Chester took possession of it.

"Well," he said, "I'm going out and ask Mr. and Mrs. Jennings if they care to make a statement. I'm going to ask them if they object if I take a look around—not that that will do any good because I understand you've already convinced yourselves the press isn't there."

"The press certainly isn't where it was when I saw it," Norda Allison said firmly.

Inspector Chester got to his feet. "Well, I'll go look around."

"Will you let us know if you find anything?" Mason asked.

The inspector smiled and shook his head. "I report to my superiors."

"But Miss Allison is an interested party," Mason said.

"All the more reason why I shouldn't report to her," Chester said, shaking hands with Mason and bowing to Norda Allison. "Thanks for the information. I'll check on it."

"Now what?" Norda Allison asked when Inspector Chester had left.

"Now," Mason said, "we do a little checking of our

own." He turned to Della Street. "Please ring the Drake Detective Agency and ask Paul Drake to come in."

Della nodded, went to the outer office and a moment later returned to say, "Drake said to tell you he's coming right away."

Mason said, by way of explanation to Norda Allison, "You talked with him. He's a very competent detective."

"I know. He's nice. That's how I got in touch with you. I—"

She broke off as Paul Drake's code knock sounded on the corridor door of Mason's private office.

Della Street opened the door. Paul Drake, tall, informal, loose-jointed, said, "Hi, Della," flashed Norda Allison a keen glance of professional appraisal, said, "How is everything, Miss Allison?" and then turned to Mason.

"Sit down, Paul," Mason invited.

Drake sat crosswise in the big overstuffed chair; one of the rounded arms propping up his back, his long legs draped over the other arm.

"Shoot."

"You're familiar with Norda Allison's story?"

"Up to the time she came in to see you this morning. What's happened since then?"

Mason told him.

"What do you want me to do?" Drake asked.

"Get on the job," Mason said. "Get out there and see whether the postal authorities are going to let Mr. and Mrs. Jennings give them a routine run-around, whether they're taking Norda Allison's story seriously and if they're making a search of the place.

"Visit around with the neighbors. Pretend you're getting magazine subscriptions or selling books or something of the sort at first. See if you can get some of the women gossiping."

"They'll throw a magazine salesman or a book salesman out on his ear so fast that—"

"All right," Mason said. "Tell them you're going to give away a free vacuum cleaner to families who represent the highest intellectual strata. Tell them it's sort of a house-to-house quiz show; that you're asking questions and you give a rating and that the person having the highest rating in the block gets a free vacuum cleaner or a set of dishes or something. Then ask questions to test their powers of observation. After a few routine questions you can start asking about the people next door."

Paul Drake shook his head. "*You* might be able to work a stunt like that, Perry. I couldn't. Each man has to shoot his own particular brand of ammunition—is there any reason I shouldn't tell them I'm a detective?"

Mason thought that over for a moment, then said, "No, but they'll freeze up on you as soon as they think you're a detective, won't they?"

"If I try to pump them they will," Drake said. "But let me get talking to the average housewife and tell her I'm a detective and right away she wants to know what I'm doing out there. Then I act mysterious and tell her it's something in the neighborhood. Then she invites me in, gives me a cup of tea or coffee, I get friendly with her, let it slip that it's the people next door I'm interested in, and then become very embarrassed at having let the information slip out. I make her promise she won't tell, and, as consideration for that promise, she insists that I tell her what it's all about and I start sparring, trying to keep from telling her and *she's* cross-examining *me*. I get in a few questions here and there. The first thing anyone knows she's told me all she knows, all she surmises, and has given me all the neighborhood gossip."

"Be careful you don't tell them anything that might serve as a basis for a suit for defamation of character," Mason warned.

Drake grinned. "I've been using this technique for ten years, Perry. Once a woman opens up with the neighborhood gossip she'll never repeat anything I say because I'll have her so badly involved she won't dare to peep."

"And then if she denies it?" Mason asked.

"Then," Drake said, "I have a little recording device

which looks like a hearing aid. I pretend I'm hard of hearing and wear this counterfeit hearing aid. Of course, tactics like that don't work *all* the time, but they work most of the time."

"Okay," Mason said. "Use your own technique. I want a couple of tails."

"One to each?" Drake asked.

"One to each," Mason told him.

Drake heaved himself up out of the chair. "On my way."

Mason smiled across at Norda Allison. "Well, that's the best *I* can do," he said. "Now I'll try getting back to that brief. Where are you staying?"

"The Millbrae Hotel."

"We'll call you if we learn anything," Mason told her. "In the meantime don't talk to anyone. If anyone calls on you or tries to pump you for information, say that I'm your attorney and am answering all questions."

Norda Allison gave him a grateful hand. "I don't know how I can thank you enough, Mr. Mason."

"You don't have to," Mason said. "I hope we can get the thing straightened out. We'll do the best we can."

6

■

IT WAS THREE-THIRTY IN THE AFTERNOON WHEN PAUL Drake called in on Mason's unlisted telephone.

Mason, who had been dictating steadily since one-thirty, regarded the ringing telephone with annoyance. He picked up the receiver, said, "Hello, Paul, what is it?"

Drake's voice over the wire said, "I have an idea you better get out here, Perry."

"Where's here?"

"Next door to the Jennings' house."

"What's it all about?" Mason asked.

Drake, speaking guardedly, said, "I'm visiting with a Mr. and Mrs. Jonathan Gales. The address is 6283 Penrace Street. They have some information that I'd like to have you check. I think you'd like to get their story."

Mason said irritably, "Now listen, Paul, I'm terribly busy at the moment. I got Della to give up her week end in order to get this dictation out and we're right in the middle of a very important matter.

"If you've uncovered any information there, write out a statement and get them to sign it. Get—"

"Then you're going to be out," Drake interrupted. "How soon can you get here, Perry?"

Mason thought that over, said into the phone, "I take it you're where you can't talk freely, Paul."

"That's right."

"How about leaving the house and going to a telephone booth where you can tell me what it's all about?"

"That might not be advisable."

"You have some information that's important?"

"Yes."

"About that printing press or something?"

"About the bloodstains," Drake said.

"About the what?"

"The bloodstains," Drake said. "You see, Perry, the postal authorities started an investigation and then after they found this gun under the pillow of the bed where Norda Allison had been sleeping, they called in the local police. She's been taken to Headquarters for questioning. For some reason the authorities are hot on her trail.

"Now, Jonathan Gales knows something about the bloodstains that I think you should know. There's some evidence here that you'd better get hold of before the police—"

"I'll be right out," Mason interrupted.

"Don't come in your car," Drake warned. "Get a taxicab, let it go as soon as you get to the house. I have an agency car out here that is rather inconspicuous. I'll drive you back when you're ready to leave."

"I'll be right out," Mason promised.

He dropped the telephone into the cradle, said to Della Street, "That's the worst of this damned office work. It gets your mind all cluttered up with stuff—I should have known the minute Drake telephoned and asked me to come out that it was important, but I had my mind so geared to trivia that I forced his hand and made him tell me what it was he considered so important. Now, the witnesses may decide to clam up."

"What was it?" she asked.

"I'll tell you in the taxi," Mason said. "Come on, let's go. The address is 6283 Penrace Street. Apparently that's next door to where the Jennings live. Grab a shorthand book and we'll take a cab. Hurry!"

They raced down the corridor to the elevator, found a cab waiting at the cabstand at the corner, climbed in and Mason gave the address.

"Now tell me what it's all about," Della Street said.

"Bloodstains," Mason told her.

"I heard you say that over the telephone. What's the significance of the bloodstains?"

"Apparently," Mason said, "the police have been called in. They found a gun under the pillow where Norda Allison had been sleeping. You remember she told about having found an ejected empty cartridge case in front of the tent where Robert was sleeping out in the patio. Now, apparently, bloodstains enter into the picture, and from the way Paul Drake talked, I have an idea the police don't know anything about those stains *as yet*."

"Well," Della Street said, *"we* seem to be getting into something."

"We seem to already have gotten into it," Mason told her, "up to our necks."

Mason lapsed into frowning concentration. Della Street, glancing at him from time to time, knowing the lawyer's habits of thought, refrained from interruption.

The cab pulled up in front of the address on Penrace Street.

"Want me to wait?" the driver asked.

Mason shook his head, handed him a five-dollar bill, said, "Keep the change."

The cabby thanked him.

Mason glanced briefly at the police car which was parked next door at the Jennings' house, walked rapidly up the cement walk to a front porch and extended his thumb toward the bell button.

The front door was opened by Paul Drake while Mason's thumb was still a good three inches from the bell button.

"Come on in," Drake said. "I was waiting at the door hoping against hope you wouldn't drive up until after Lieutenant Tragg had left."

"That's Tragg over in the other house?" Mason asked.

Drake nodded, said, "Come on in and meet the folks."

Drake led the way into a cozy living room which had an air of comfortable simplicity.

There were deep chairs, comfortable in appearance, books, a large table, a television set, floor lamps conveniently arranged by the chairs, newspapers and magazines on the table. Through an archway could be seen a dining room with a big sideboard, a glass-enclosed cupboard for dishes. The house itself was modern, but the furniture gave the impression of being comfortably old-fashioned without qualifying for the label of "antique."

A somewhat elderly couple arose as Paul Drake escorted Mason and Della Street into the living room.

"This is Mr. and Mrs. Gales," Paul Drake said by way of introduction. "They have quite a story; at least Mr. Gales has."

Gales, a tall, bleached individual with a drooping moustache, bushy white eyebrows and gray eyes, extended a bony hand to Perry Mason. "Well, well," he said, "I'm certainly pleased to meet *you!* I've read a lot about you, but never thought I'd be seeing you—Martha and I don't get out much any more and we spend a lot of time reading. I guess Martha has followed every one of your cases."

Mrs. Gales reached out to take Della Street's hand. "And I've seen photographs of Miss Street," she said. "I'm really a fan of yours, my dear, as well as of Mr. Mason. Now, do sit down and if we can do anything that will be of any help, we're only too glad to do it.

"How about making a cup of tea? I could . . ."

Drake glanced at his wrist watch, then looked significantly through the windows over towards the Jennings' house. He said, "We may be interrupted at any minute, Mrs. Gales. If you don't mind, I'd like to have you tell your story just as briefly as possible—what you have to say about Robert."

"Well, do sit down," she said. "Let's be comfortable. Heavens to Betsy, I certainly feel shoddy having people like you here and not being able to offer a cup of tea. I've got some nice cookies I baked yesterday—"

"About the gun," Drake said. "Tell Mr. Mason about Robert and the gun."

"Well, there's not much to tell. Robert is a mighty nice, very well-behaved boy. But he's just crazy about guns. He's always watching those Western television shows— 'pistol pictures,' Jonathan calls them.

"They have a baby sitter over there who takes care of him when Mr. and Mrs. Jennings go out, and I've noticed that when the baby sitter is there Robert has a *real* gun to play with."

"A real gun?" Mason asked.

"An automatic," Jonathan Gales supplemented. "Looks like a Colt Woodsman model. I think it's a .22 caliber."

"He only has that when the baby sitter is there?" Mason asked.

"Well, now, that's the only time I've *seen* him with it," Mrs. Gales said, "but if you ask me, a seven-year-old boy has got no business playing around with a real pistol . . . personally, I think it's bad enough when they start pulling

43

these imitation six-shooters out of holsters, pointing them at people and saying, 'Bang! Bang! You're dead!' Good heavens! When I was a girl, if my brother had even pointed a cap pistol at anybody, my dad would have warmed him up good and proper.

"Nowadays, boys go around with these toy pistols and think nothing of pointing them at somebody and saying, 'Boom! You're dead!' You can see what it's doing. Pick up the paper almost any day and you see where some child ten, twelve or fifteen years old killed off a parent because he was mad at not being allowed to go to a movie. I don't know what the world's coming to when—"

"Do you know who this baby sitter is?" Paul Drake interposed.

"No, I don't. They have a couple of them. This one I'm talking about has only been working there about six weeks. The Jennings aren't much for being neighborly, and. . . . Well, this is a peculiar neighborhood. People seem to live pretty much to themselves.

"Time was when people used to swap a little gossip and borrow things back and forth, but now there's a car in the garage and whenever they have a minute they get up and scoot off someplace. Then when they're home they're watching television or something. Seems like times are changing right under our eyes."

"This baby sitter," Mason prompted, "an older or a younger woman?"

"The one who lets him have the gun is an older woman —oh, I'd say somewhere in the forties." She laughed. "Of course, that's not old at all, you understand. It's just that she's older than the other one, and, of course, older than some of the baby sitters they have these days; girls going to high school who come and sit with kids for an evening. I don't know what would happen if there was any sort of an emergency. I don't know what one of those girls could do."

"Well, as far as that's concerned, what could a woman

44

of forty-five do?" Jonathan Gales commented. "Suppose some man walked in, and—"

"We have to hurry along," Drake interrupted, his voice apologetic. "I would like to have Mr. Mason hear your story just the way you told it to me. We'll have time only for highlights. You've seen the child playing with this automatic?"

Mrs. Gales nodded emphatically.

"How about you?" Drake asked, turning to Jonathan Gales.

"I've seen him two or three times," Jonathan Gales said. "The very first time I saw it, I said to Martha, 'It looks to me like that kid's got a real gun over there,' and Martha said, 'No, it can't be. That's just some kind of a wooden gun. They're making imitations these days that look so much like the real thing they scare a body to death.'

"Well, I took a good, long second look at it and I said, 'Martha, I'm betting that's a real gun,' and sure enough, it was."

"Did you ever have it in your hands?" Mason asked.

"No, but I did think enough about it to get my binoculars and take a look at it—Martha and I do a little bird watching out in the backyard and we've got a mighty good pair of binoculars, coated lenses and all. They're sharp as a tack."

"All right," Drake said, hurrying things along. "The child at times plays with a real gun. You've noticed that only when this one baby sitter was there."

They both nodded.

"Now, about the bloodstains," Drake said.

"Well, that's the thing I can't understand," Gales said. "This morning Barton Jennings was up before daylight. He went someplace. Then, later on, he had a hose and he was out there washing off the sidewalk and pretending he was watering the lawn. It wasn't five-thirty.

"Now, of course, that's not unusually early for people that are accustomed to getting up early, but over there in the Jennings house they like to sleep late—you take on a Saturday or a Sunday when they aren't going anywhere they'll stay in bed until nine-ten o'clock in the morning. You'll see Robert up playing around by himself out there in the patio."

"Not that we're the nosy kind," Martha Gales interposed, "but we do our bird watching, a lot of it, in the morning. That's when birds are moving around and both Jonathan and I are early risers. There's a hedge between the properties, but you can see through it if someone is moving around. If anybody over there is sitting still-like, it isn't easy to see him. But if a body's moving around over in the patio in the Jennings' house you can see sort of a shadowy outline through the leaves in the hedge."

"Jennings was watering the lawn?" Mason prompted.

"Well, it wasn't so much watering the lawn," Gales said, "as hosing it off. He was *pretending* to water the lawn but he was holding the hose almost straight down and walking it along the lawn, using too much force to just be watering the grass. He was putting the full stream of water along a narrow strip—oh, maybe two or three feet wide—walking right along with it. Then he came to the sidewalk and he hosed off the sidewalk and in a couple of places I saw him put the nozzle right down within eighteen inches of the cement, just like he was trying to wash something away.

"Well, I didn't think too much of it until I went out to get my paper. The delivery boy had tossed the paper and usually he tosses it right up on the porch. This morning it didn't seem to be on the porch and I went out looking for it and I found it in the gutter. Evidently it had slipped out of the delivery boy's hand. It looks like there had been blood in that water that ran down the gutter."

"You have the paper?" Drake asked.

Gales handed the newspaper to Mason. "Now, it was rolled up this way," he explained, rolling up the front page, "and then there was a rubber elastic band around it. You can see the water had quite a reddish tinge to it."

"But what makes you think it's blood?" Mason asked.

"I'm coming to that," Gales said. "When I went out looking for the paper, Jennings was just finishing up watering along the sidewalk. I said to him, 'Good morning' and told him it looked like it was going to be a nice day, just sort of neighborly-like, and he seemed right startled to see me out there. And, before he thought, he said sharply, 'What are *you* looking for?' Well, I told him I was looking for my newspaper; that it wasn't on the porch or on the front lawn and sometimes when the boy threw it out of the car it would hit against the side of the car door and drop down in the gutter. So then I looked down in the gutter and said, 'Here it is; right here in the gutter.'

"I picked it up and Jennings said, 'Gosh, I hope I didn't get it wet. I was watering the lawn.' Well, I looked at it and saw it was wet all right, but I said, 'Oh, well, it'll dry right out. It isn't very wet; just the corner. You're up early this morning, aren't you?'

"Well, he said he'd had to take Robert and the dog out someplace to meet with some other boys that were going out on a camping trip, and then I saw his eyes rest on the paper I was holding. Something in the expression of his eyes caused me to look down, and I could see there was this reddish stain on the paper. Well, I didn't say a word, but I brought the paper in and dried it out, and Martha and I had our cup of coffee. We both like a cup of coffee first thing in the morning and then we read the newspaper. Sometimes we don't actually get around to breakfast for an hour or two. We sit out in the yard and watch birds and maybe sip coffee, and——"

"There was a bloodstain," Drake said.

"That's right. I'm coming to that. I got to thinking about the reddish color on the paper, and along about ten or eleven o'clock I could see there was a lot of unusual activity over there at the Jennings' house, with people coming and going, so I got to wondering about the way he'd been washing off that sidewalk with the hose. You see, he quit doing that the minute I got out there. He acted just as if he'd been a kid that had been caught in some kind of mischief. Well, I went out to look around. Out there in the gutter, just alongside the curb above where the paper had been lying, there was a red blotch of blood that hadn't been washed away yet. I'm pretty sure it was blood, and out a little ways from the curb you could see two spots of blood—looked like somebody had been bleeding and had left the place, walking along the lawn instead of along the walk and then stood for a minute at the gutter, getting a car door open, then had stepped into the car and driven away.

"Now, you probably think I'm . . . well, maybe you'll think I'm a little mite too nosy or something, but I just got to wondering about that blood. I said to Martha, I said, 'Martha, suppose that seven-year-old kid was playing with a gun? Suppose they let him have it and took the shells out of it whenever he was playing with it, but suppose this time they didn't get *all* the shells out. Suppose there happened to be a shell left in the barrel and suppose he'd shot somebody?' "

"Anything that makes you think he did?" Mason asked.

Gales hesitated for a moment, then slowly shook his head. "Nothing in particular—nothing I can put my finger on."

"Don't be so cautious, Jonathan," Martha Gales prompted. "Why don't you go ahead and tell them what you told *me?*"

"Because I can't prove anything and I may be getting in pretty deep."

"Go ahead," Drake said impatiently, "let's have it."

"Well, of course, it's only just a surmise, but Robert was going out on some kind of a Scout trip or something this morning—now why in the world would anyone get up to take a kid out on a Scout trip at four o'clock in the morning—and *I* thought I heard a shot sometime last night."

Mason and Drake exchanged glances.

48

"They took Robert out at four o'clock in the morning?" Mason asked.

Gales nodded. "Must have been around there. It was before daylight."

"If you couldn't see, how did you know it was Robert?"

"I heard them talking. I didn't look at the time, but it must have been right around four o'clock."

"And it was after Robert left that you saw Jennings washing off the sidewalk?"

"That's right."

"His arthritis is bothering him this morning, I believe," Mason said.

"Yes, he had his cane with him this morning."

Drake, looking out of the window, said, "Oh-oh, here comes Lieutenant Tragg."

Mason said to Jonathan Gales, "All right, tell me about the baby sitter. What do you know about her? Does she drive her own car?"

"That's right."

"What make is it?"

"I can't tell you the make. It's an older type of car—a sedan."

"She's in her forties?"

"I would say so."

"Heavy-set?"

"Well, not fat, just . . . well, rather broad across the beam."

"How long has she been baby-sitting for them?"

"Well, I guess maybe six-eight weeks or so. Robert is only there for part time. You know, he's a child by another marriage—Selkirk, his name is, and—"

The doorbell sounded.

Martha Gales said, "I'll get it."

"Never mind Robert," Mason said. "I know all about him. I'm interested in this baby sitter. Do they say anything about her, or . . ."

"No, we don't visit much back and forth. I—"

"You don't think she's some relative, or . . . ?"

49

"No, I think they got her through an agency. I think they said—"

Lieutenant Tragg's voice said, "How do you do, madam. I'm Lieutenant Tragg of the homicide department. I'm making an investigation and I'd like to ask you a few questions. Do you mind if I come in?"

Tragg didn't wait for an answer but pushed his way into the interior of the house, then jerked back in surprise as he saw Mason, Della Street and Paul Drake.

"Well, well, well," he said, "what brings all of *you* here?"

"What brings *you* here?" Mason countered.

Tragg hesitated a moment, then said, "Well, you'll read it in the papers so I guess there's no harm in telling you. Mervin Selkirk was found dead in his automobile in the parking lot of the San Sebastian Country Club shortly after one o'clock this afternoon. He'd been dead for some time. There'd been an extensive hemorrhage from a chest wound. The doors of the car were closed and the windows were all up. The fatal bullet was of .22 caliber and there's reason to believe it was fired from a Colt automatic."

Lieutenant Tragg looked at the horrified faces of Martha and Jonathan Gales. "You folks know anything about Mervin Selkirk?" he asked. "Ever meet him? Know him when you see him? Did you see him here last night?"

They shook their heads.

"We don't know him," Gales said.

"Anything unusual take place next door during the night?" Tragg asked. "The boy, Robert, was Mervin Selkirk's son, you know."

Martha Gales shook her head.

Jonathan Gales said, "Not that we know of. The only thing I know about is the bloodstains."

Lieutenant Tragg snapped to attention as though he had received an unexpected jolt of an electric current. "Bloodstains! Where?"

"Next door and on the sidewalk. I was telling Mr. Mason, his secretary and Mr. Drake here about what we saw—"

Tragg said, "Hold it, hold it! Okay, Mason, I guess you've beaten me to it, but from now on we'll follow standard procedure. We'll excuse you. This is a police investigation of a murder."

As Mason hesitated, Tragg added, "We can, of course, just take these people up to the district attorney's office and interrogate them there, but it will be more convenient for all of us if we do it here. And," he added with a wry smile, "if you're as fast as you usually are, you already have all the information you need."

Mason shook hands with Mr. and Mrs. Gales. "Thanks for your co-operation," he said. "You'll find Lieutenant Tragg likes to adopt a hard-boiled exterior. He barks and he growls, but he really doesn't bite."

"On your way," Tragg said gruffly.

Mason led the way to the door.

"I'll drive you folks to the office," Drake said, as he held open the door of his car.

"No, you won't," Mason said. "There isn't time for that. Drive us to the nearest taxi stand, then get out to the San Sebastian Country Club, find out everything you can dig up out there. I also want you to locate the Selkirk boy. I want to interview him. You'd better telephone your office, and, while you're about it, tell them to find out who the Jennings' baby sitter is."

"That's like looking for a needle in a haystack," Drake protested.

"No, it isn't, Paul," Mason said. "We don't give a damn about the haystack, so that will help. Burn up the haystack and wash away the ashes. That will leave the needle where you can find it. It's the needle we're interested in, not the haystack. Now, get busy."

7

MASON FOLLOWED DELLA STREET INTO THE ELEVATOR, said, "Well, I guess the day is all shot to pieces now."

Della laughed. "And how you enjoy it! You hate routine work and whenever any excuse comes up that enables you to break away from office work and dictation you're as pleased as a seven-year-old kid who has just learned that the schoolhouse has burned down."

Mason grinned at Della Street's comment. The assistant janitor who operated one of the elevators on Saturday afternoons said, "I think you've got someone waiting to see you, Mr. Mason." He brought the cage to a stop, still holding the door closed.

Mason frowned.

"He came up about half an hour ago. I told him you weren't in and he'd have to sign the register to get in on Saturday afternoon, unless he was going to one of the offices that were regularly open on a twenty-four-hour basis, such as the Drake Detective Agency."

"What did he say?" Mason asked.

"He looked me right in the eye and said he was really intending to go to the Drake Detective Agency; that he'd simply asked about you on the off-chance you might be in your office. I think he was lying."

"Okay," Mason said. "We can turn him down fast."

"And hard," Della Street amended.

The janitor slid the doors open. Mason and Della Street stepped out into the corridor.

A man who had been standing just beside the door of the Drake Detective Agency said, "Are you Mr. Mason?"

Mason regarded him without cordiality. "I'm Mr. Mason," he said. "It's Saturday. My secretary has sacrificed her week end in order to help me get out some emergency work and I'm not seeing clients."

The man, who seemed to be having some difficulty with his speech, said, "This is an emergency, Mr. Mason. It has to do with Miss Norda Allison. It's very important."

Mason regarded the man sharply. "All right," he said, "I'll let you come in. You'll have to be brief."

The three of them walked in silence down the echoing corridor of the building, turned at the door of Mason's private office. Mason unlatched the door, held it open for Della Street and his visitor, then followed them in, seated himself behind the desk, said, "All right, let's have it."

"I'm Nathan Benedict," the man said. "I have known Miss Allison for some time. I knew about her . . . her attachment for Mervin Selkirk—Selkirk broke my jaw."

"Oh, yes," Mason said. "And what are you doing down here, Mr. Benedict?"

Benedict started to say something, then seemed momentarily unable to speak. When he had recovered himself, he said, "You're going to have to make allowances, Mr. Mason. My jaw gives me a little trouble yet—not so much the bones as the muscles."

Mason nodded.

"I came down here to protect Norda Allison," Benedict said. "I think a great deal of her. This Selkirk is a dangerous man, Mr. Mason; an absolutely dangerous man. I know from experience."

Mason sat silently contemplating his visitor while Della Street took rapid notes in her shorthand book.

"Selkirk deliberately attacked me," Benedict went on. "He thrust his foot out as I walked across the floor, then jumped up, yelled, 'Who are you pushing?' and pulled his fist, with the brass knuckles already in place, out of his pocket. He hit me a terrific blow, then stepped back and slipped the brass knuckles to one of his acquaintances."

53

"Any idea who those friends of his were?" Mason asked.

"One of them remained and gave his name to the police. The other seemed to fade out of the picture. I think it was the other one who took the brass knuckles away with him."

"You don't know his name?"

Benedict shook his head.

"All right," Mason said, "in view of developments I think we can find who that man was, and it's vitally important to find out something about him.

"Della."

Della Street looked up from her notebook.

"As soon as Mr. Benedict leaves," Mason said, "contact Paul Drake. Tell him we want the complete low-down on that altercation in the bar in which Mr. Benedict was injured; we want the names of the people who were with Selkirk, and we want to interview them before the police do. I want to find out something about those brass knuckles.

"All right, Benedict, go ahead. What's the rest of it?"

"Well, that's all there is," Benedict said. "I knew Norda Allison was coming down here to see Lorraine Jennings, who was Selkirk's first wife. I have an idea they're trying to get Norda mixed up in a fight over the custody of the child. If she gets mixed up in that, I *know* she'll be in danger."

"How did you happen to come to me?" Mason asked.

"I rang up the Jennings' residence a while ago. Jennings answered the phone. I told him it was important that I speak with Norda. I was told she wasn't there. Jennings seemed rather frigidly formal about it, too. I suppose he doesn't understand my motives.

"He told me that if I wanted to know anything about Norda Allison I would have to get in touch with you; that you were the only one who could give me any information."

"And what made you think I would be at my office this afternoon?"

"Jennings said he thought you were here, or would be here later."

"I see," Mason said thoughtfully. "And Jennings didn't seem to be cordial?"

"He was very cool over the telephone. Of course, I can't blame him. I suppose Norda will be angry, too."

"When did you arrive here in this city?" Mason asked.

"Last night, about ten-thirty."

"How did you know Miss Allison was here?"

"I drove her to the airport."

"And then?"

"I saw her on the plane, then went and purchased a ticket and took the next plane."

"And then?"

"I rented a car at the airport."

"And then?"

Benedict cleared his throat. "I drove out to the Jennings' place to keep watch."

Mason glanced over at Della Street's busy pen. "What happened—if anything?"

"I was watching the house. Foolishly, I was smoking. A prowl car drove past. The officers saw the glowing tip of the cigarette. They went on by. An hour later they came cruising by again and asked me what I was waiting for. They made me show them my driving license and told me to get out of the neighborhood and go to bed.

"I felt terribly humiliated, but I went to a motel. About eight-thirty I rang the Jennings residence and asked for Norda. I was told she was still asleep. I left word for her to call and left my number."

"Then what?" Mason asked.

"Then I waited and waited. When she hadn't called by midafternoon I was afraid she was angry. I felt I'd messed things up some way. I called again an hour or so ago and that was when Jennings said I'd have to see you."

"I see," Mason said thoughtfully. "Just how did you propose to protect Miss Allison, Mr. Benedict?"

"I don't know, but I intend to protect her."

Mason said, "You're not particularly robust physically and in dealing with Mervin Selkirk you would have been dealing with a cold-blooded, ruthless individual who would stop at nothing. You have already had one contact from which you emerged second best."

Benedict nodded, tight-lipped.

"Yet you say you intend to protect Norda Allison?"

"Yes."

"How?"

"Well, if you must know," Benedict said, "in my position I sometimes have occasion to carry large sums of money. I have a permit to carry a weapon, and—"

"Let's see it," Mason said.

Benedict frowned and hesitated.

"Come on," Mason said, "let's see it."

Benedict reached inside of his coat and pulled a revolver from a shoulder holster. He placed it on the table.

"A .38-caliber, lightweight Colt revolver," Mason said. He picked it up, swung open the cylinder, inspected the shells and then added, "It is now fully loaded."

Mason smelled the barrel. "Either it has not been fired recently or it has been cleaned after it was fired."

"May I ask what causes your detailed scrutiny?" Benedict inquired. "You're acting rather strangely, Mr. Mason."

Mason said, "For your information, Mervin Selkirk was shot and fatally wounded. He died in his automobile out at the San Sebastian Country Club. As yet, I don't know the exact time of death. You say you have a permit to carry this gun?"

Benedict said with widened eyes, "You mean Mervin Selkirk is dead?"

"He's dead," Mason said. "Murdered. You say you have a permit to carry this gun. Let's see it."

As one in a daze, Benedict extracted a wallet from his pocket, took out a sheet of paper which had been folded and bore evidences of having been carried for some period of time.

Mason studied the permit, then looked at the number on the gun.

"Well," he said, "they check. I would suggest that you board the first plane, go back to San Francisco, go about your regular routine business and forget you were ever down here."

"But Norda. Where's Norda?" Benedict asked.

"As nearly as I can find out," Mason said, "she is either at police headquarters or at the district attorney's office. She's probably being questioned, but she *may* have been booked on suspicion of murder."

"Norda!" Benedict exclaimed. "Murder!"

"That's right."

"But I can't understand! I can't . . . it simply isn't possible."

"What isn't possible?"

"That Norda killed him."

"I didn't say she killed him," Mason said. "I said she might have been booked on suspicion of murder. Now, I'm not in a position to advise you. I'm representing her. Speaking not as an attorney but just as a person who would like to be your friend, I suggest that having learned there's nothing you can do to protect Norda from Mervin Selkirk, you return to San Francisco."

Benedict shook his head. "I'm sorry, Mr. Mason, but I can't do that. I'm going to have to stay here now to see if there is anything I can do.

"Mr. Mason, I . . . I'm employed on a salary, but I have made some rather fortunate investments. I am a bachelor, I have saved my money, and if . . . well, I'll be perfectly frank with you, Mr. Mason. In all, I have nearly forty thousand dollars in the bank. I would be prepared to assist Norda financially if that is necessary."

"We'll find out about that after a while," Mason said, "but you can assist her financially from San Francisco as well as from down here."

"No," Benedict said. "I intend to remain here."

"You remain here," Mason said angrily, "and not only

will the police pick you up and shake you down but if they crowd my client, I'll lower the boom on you myself. It's not my duty to help the police solve murders. It's my duty to protect my clients. But right now you're about the best murder suspect I could dig up, if I had to provide a good red herring."

Benedict thought that over for a moment, then his face lit up. "Mr. Mason, that's exactly the thing to do! If anyone intimates Norda killed him, you can use me as a red herring. In that way I can help . . . will Norda be able to have visitors? I mean can I talk with her?"

"Not for a while," Mason said, "not if they charge her with murder."

"But *you* can see her as her attorney?"

"Yes."

"Tell her I'm here," Benedict said. "Tell her what I told you about having funds available to help her financially."

"You stick around here," Mason said, "and keep packing that gun, and I won't need to tell her anything about you. She'll pick up the newspaper and read *all* about you. You'll have your photograph published with headlines to the effect that police questioned Mervin Selkirk's broken-jawed rival and found him carrying what may have been the murder weapon."

"That certainly makes it sound sensational," Benedict said.

"Well, what did you expect?"

"If," Benedict said with dignity, "the police are no more efficient in locating me than they were in locating the brass knuckles which Mervin Selkirk used in breaking my jaw, they'll *never* know I'm here."

Mason said, "In the one instance you were dealing with a barroom altercation over a woman. Now you're dealing with murder. You'll find there's a difference. Now let me ask you one other thing. Do you by any chance own any other weapon, say, for instance, a .22 automatic?"

"Why yes, I do, but I only carry that on fishing trips,

as a protection against snakes and to kill grouse for camp meat."

"Where is that gun now?"

"At my apartment in San Francisco."

"You're certain?"

Benedict hesitated.

"Well?" Mason prompted.

"No," Benedict said. "I can't *swear* to it. I looked for it yesterday afternoon; I wanted to bring it with me. I couldn't find it. I suppose I put it . . . well, I didn't make any search. I just looked in the drawer where I usually keep both guns. The .38 was there, the .22 wasn't."

Benedict's eyes searched Mason's face. "I'm afraid you're attaching too much emphasis to a fact which has no real significance, Mr. Mason. The gun's around my apartment somewhere. I'm a bachelor and not much of a housekeeper. Things get scattered around some. I . . . come to think of it, I may have left it rolled up in the sleeping bag I used on a fishing trip two months ago. I love to fish."

Mason studied the man.

"I want to know more about this charge against Norda," Benedict said. "I don't see how anyone on earth could possibly suspect that . . ."

He broke off as knuckles pounded authoritatively on the exit door leading from Mason's private office to the corridor.

After a moment the knock was repeated.

Mason pushed back his chair, walked over to the door, called out, "Who is it?"

"Lieutenant Tragg," came the voice from the other side. "Open up. We're looking for Nathan Benedict. He's supposed to be in your office."

Mason opened the door. "Hello, Tragg. Meet Nathan Benedict," he said.

Lieutenant Tragg said, "How are you, Benedict? When did you get in?"

"You mean here in the office?"

"Here in the city."

"By plane last night."

"What time?"

"I arrived about ten-thirty."

"Where?"

"At the International Airport."

"Where did you go from there?"

"I rented a car and drove out to Barton Jennings' house. I wanted to see Norda Allison. She'd evidently retired. I sat there for a while, then went to a motel."

"What motel?" Tragg asked.

"The Restwell."

"Then what?"

"This morning I tried to call Norda Allison. I left my number."

Tragg eyed him narrowly.

Mason said, "For your information, Lieutenant, since I am not representing Mr. Benedict and the information which he gave me was volunteered and not on a confidential basis, he came down here to protect Norda Allison from Mervin Selkirk. He knew that he was unable to resist Selkirk on a physical basis, so he carried along a .38-caliber Colt lightweight revolver for which he seems to have a permit which is perfectly in order."

"Well, what do you know about that!" Tragg said. "Where's the gun?"

Benedict reached inside of his coat.

"Bring it out slow," Lieutenant Tragg warned, stepping forward. "Put it down on the desk with the butt toward me and the end of the barrel pointed toward you."

Benedict placed the gun on the desk.

Lieutenant Tragg picked it up, snapped open the cylinder, looked at the shells, smelled the barrel, snapped the cylinder shut, put the gun in his pocket.

"All right, Benedict," he said, "you and I are going to have a nice little talk, and since Mr. Mason isn't your attorney and since he has a lot of work to do, we'll just move on and let Mr. Mason get back to his work."

"But I don't *have* to go with you," Benedict said, drawing himself up.

Lieutenant Tragg's mouth clamped into a thin, firm line. "That's what *you* think," he said. "Come on."

At the door Tragg turned and said over his shoulder to Mason, "I was prepared for Benedict here to offer himself as a sheep for the slaughter, but hardly prepared to have you drive him into the killing pen for us quite so soon."

Mason sighed wearily. "I try to co-operate and that's all the thanks I get."

Tragg said thoughtfully, "When you co-operate you do it so willingly, so damned eagerly. And this guy might even go so far as to put on an act just to take the heat off his girl friend—with a little coaching from you, of course."

Mason said angrily, "You might also ask him if he happens to own a .22 Colt automatic."

"If you think we won't, you're crazy," Tragg said, "but we might not believe all his answers. The D.A. gets suspicious of the Greeks when they bring gifts—of red herring!

"Come on, Benedict, you're worth looking into, even if we are going to listen to any admissions you may make with skeptical ears."

Tragg took Benedict firmly by the elbow and escorted him out into the corridor.

The automatic door check slowly closed the door and clicked it shut.

Mason and Della Street exchanged glances.

"Well," Della Street said, "shall we go on with our dictation?"

Mason made an expression of distaste, looked at his wrist watch and said, "For your information, Miss Street, we are not going on with any dictation. This man, Benedict, has turned out to be a confusing element which raises the devil with my desire to concentrate on dictation. In order to show you my sincerity in determining not to work on any more details, I hereby invite you out for a cocktail and a nice steak dinner."

"And afterward?" she asked.

"Afterward," Mason said, "we might look around some of the nightspots and do a little dancing, if that appeals to you."

"And the brief?" she asked.

"Under the circumstances," Mason said, "I'll go into court Monday morning, explain the emergency which arose over the week end and get a week's extension."

"Under those circumstances," Della Street said, "my duty is perfectly obvious. Shall we stop by Paul Drake's office and tell him to look up the San Francisco brass knuckles affair?"

Mason shook his head. "No," he said, "there's no use now. Tragg will shake Benedict down at police headquarters. Newspaper reporters will eagerly pounce on him as a sensational development in the Selkirk murder. Tragg will let them take pictures. They'll call the San Francisco newspapers. The San Francisco papers will start ace reporters trying to cover the local angle of the case, and tomorrow morning's paper will have the names of the men who were with Selkirk in the cocktail lounge. By that time, police will have interviewed both of the men and probably exerted considerable pressure to find out about the brass knuckles.

"There's no use paying out our client's money to get information we can read in the newspaper."

"But is there any chance Paul Drake's men could get to these men first, and——"

Mason smiled and shook his head. "Don't underestimate the San Francisco newspaper reporters, Della—and while you're about it, don't underestimate the San Francisco police.

"Come on, let's go get those cocktails."

"Plural?" Della Street asked.

"Two," Mason said, "and then dinner."

8

Della Street, looking up from her plate, said "Oh-oh, I think we're going to have company, Chief."

Mason, who particularly detested having persons who recognized him in restaurants and night clubs come barging up with excuses to get acquainted or to present some legal problem, tightened his lips.

"Right behind you," Della Street said, "walking very purposefully toward you. He chatted with the waiter for a minute and . . . oh-oh, here comes Fred, the manager."

"Good for Fred," Mason said.

"Fred's intercepted him," Della Street said. "Relax, he'll be on his way out in a moment."

Della Street cut off another piece of her steak, raised the bite halfway to her lips, then paused, frowning.

"What now?" Mason asked.

"He evidently has some influence," Della Street said. "Fred's coming over."

A moment later the manager bent over Mason's chair. "Mr. Mason, I know how you dislike to be disturbed. I dislike very much to do this, but—"

"Don't do it then," Mason snapped.

"It's not that simple," Fred said apologetically. "Mr. Selkirk, Horace Livermore Selkirk, the banker, insists that he's going to talk with you. I headed him off. Then he suggested that I come and ask your permission but . . . well, you know how it is. We appreciate your patronage enormously, Mr. Mason, and we try to respect your desire for privacy but we're hardly in a position to give Horace Selkirk the old heave ho."

Mason hesitated for a moment. "I see your problem,

Fred," he said. "All right. Tell Mr. Selkirk that I'll make an exception in his case."

"Thanks a million, Mr. Mason!" the manager exclaimed in relief. "Gosh, Mr. Mason, you don't know what a load you've taken off of my shoulders. I was afraid I was going to have to go back and . . . well, I have a loan with Mr. Selkirk's bank. He put me in a very embarrassing position."

"Does he know you have the loan?" Mason asked, grinning.

"He didn't," Fred said, grinning, "but he will very shortly after I go back to him."

Mason laughed outright. "Go ahead, Fred, spread it on as thick as you want. I'll see him but I don't think the interview will be very satisfactory to him."

"That's not in my department," the manager said. "Emily Post's book on etiquette says that when you owe a bank twenty thousand dollars it's not considered exactly proper to ask two waiters to escort the president of that bank to the door."

The manager moved back to Selkirk, and Della Street, watching what was going on with keen interest, said, "I'll bet Fred *is* spreading it on thick—well, here they come."

Fred led Selkirk over to the table. "Mr. Mason," he said, "I wish to present Horace Livermore Selkirk, the president of the bank with which I do business. I certainly will appreciate anything you can do for Mr. Selkirk as a personal favor and I do want to tell you, Mr. Mason, how very deeply I appreciate your granting me the personal favor of giving Mr. Selkirk an interview. I know your unfailing policy in regard to privacy."

Mason shook hands with Horace Selkirk, said, "This is Miss Street, my secretary, Mr. Selkirk. Would you care to be seated?"

The manager deferentially held a chair and Selkirk dropped into it.

"A drink?" Mason asked.

"No, thanks."

"You've dined?"

"Yes, thank you."

"Anything we can do for you?" the manager asked.

"Nothing," Selkirk said crisply.

The manager bowed and withdrew. Mason studied the banker, a man who had bushy white eyebrows, slate-gray eyes, a profuse mane of iron-gray hair, and a mouth which indicated he was accustomed to getting his own way.

"I take it," Mason said, "you wish to consult me on a matter of some importance."

"That's right. My own time is exceedingly valuable, Mr. Mason. I can assure you that I wouldn't waste it on a trivial matter even if I wanted to waste yours."

"May I ask how you happened to locate me here?" Mason said curiously.

"I get information the same way you do, Mr. Mason."

Mason raised his eyebrows.

"I feel that information is the most important ammunition a man can have to fire at an adversary in a business deal. Therefore I try to have accurate authentic information and I try to get it fast. There are specialists in the field of getting information just as there are specialists in the field of law and in the field of banking. I have the best detective agency I can get and when I put it to work I get results."

Mason studied the other man thoughtfully. "Am I to assume that detectives have been shadowing me during the day so that you could put your finger on me at any time you wanted me?"

"Not during the day. However, when you entered my affairs, I entered yours. You can be assured that when I wanted you, I knew where to find you and that whenever I want to know where to find you in the future I will be able to do so with the briefest delay possible."

"All right," Mason told him. "What do you want? Why go to all that trouble?"

"Because you're representing Norda Allison," Selkirk

said. "She's going to be charged with the murder of my son. I can assure you, Mr. Mason, that I intend to see that my son's murder is avenged. I don't care what I have to do, to what lengths I have to go, or how much it costs. I am going to avenge my son's death."

"Surely," Mason said, "you didn't come here simply to tell me that."

"I wanted to warn you. You are reputed to be a very resourceful and adroit attorney. You have the reputation of skating right along the thin edge of legal ethics in order to serve your clients. Frequently your ethics have been questioned but you have always managed to come up with the right answer and extricate yourself from the difficulty."

Mason said nothing.

"In those cases in the past, however," Selkirk went on, "you haven't been up against a determined, resourceful antagonist who is perhaps equally intelligent, equally adroit, and if you come right down to it, equally unscrupulous."

Mason said, "You'll pardon me, Mr. Selkirk, but I've had a busy day. I want to relax and enjoy my dinner and I'm not interested in having you come to my table in order to make threats."

"Whether you're interested or not, I'm here."

"All right," Mason told him. "You've stated your position. Now I'll state mine. I don't propose to have you sit at my table and keep making threats."

"I think I'm in control of the situation," Selkirk said. "I have a mortgage on this restaurant. There's no one here who's going to throw me out."

"Take another look," Mason said.

"Where?"

"At me. I'll throw you out."

Selkirk looked him over. "Give me a year, Mr. Mason, and I can bring about your financial ruin in this city regardless of your ability."

"Give me forty-five seconds," Mason said, pushing

back his chair, "and I'll bring about your physical ruin if you don't get the hell out of here."

Selkirk held up a restraining hand. "Calm down, Mason," he said. "You're enough of a fighter to realize you can't put up your best fight when you're angry. A prize fighter never gets mad; if he does, he loses the fight. A good lawyer puts on quite a show about being mad but if he's a topflight attorney, he is as cool as a cucumber all the time he's registering indignation.

"Now then, I may have overemphasized my initial point. I wanted to have you understand that I have a considerable amount of power. I can be a powerful enemy but, on the other hand, I can be an equally powerful friend."

"A bribe?" Mason asked coldly.

"Don't be silly," Selkirk said. "I know you wouldn't take a bribe. I'm not offering to befriend you. You don't want my friendship—now. I'm offering to befriend someone who needs it. You can't turn down the friendship for your client—a friendship and assistance I am prepared to offer."

"Under what conditions?"

"My son," Horace Selkirk said, "was a Selkirk. Therefore he had the benefit of such protection as the family could give him. I have from time to time used my influence on behalf of that boy. I have had to extricate him from rather serious situations. I know that he was not perfect. He had a nasty habit of being unfailingly polite while engaged in sadistic skirmishes.

"I'm not that way. I never skirmish. I either get along on a peaceful basis of live-and-let-live or I go to war. When I go to war I make a major campaign out of it. I destroy my enemy absolutely, ruthlessly and completely. I don't believe in halfway measures.

"I mention this, however, because I want you to know that the things my son did never met with my entire approval.

"My son was infatuated with Norda Allison. He quite

probably would have ruined her mental health before he'd have let her marry someone else. I am not contending that my son was always in the right.

"However, we now come to the main reason for my visit. That is my grandson, Robert Selkirk."

Mason's face, which had been ominously unsmiling, suddenly showed interest. "Go on," he said.

"The story the child's mother, Lorraine Jennings, and her husband, Barton Jennings, told the police was that Robert was going on a three-day camping trip. They had to take him and his dog to a place where he could join the group. They said they left him at the appointed place early this morning.

"For your private information, Mr. Mason, that is a complete fabrication. Robert did not join any group early this morning. There was no occasion for him to do so. The group was not scheduled to depart until ten-thirty. Actually it got away at eleven-twenty-two. Robert was not with the group."

"Where is he then?" Mason asked.

"Evidently he has been spirited away somewhere and is being held in concealment."

"Why?" Mason asked.

"I *thought* you might be interested in finding out why," Selkirk said.

"Go ahead," Mason said.

"It might develop into a story which would be of some interest to you as the legal representative of Norda Allison. It might result in her acquittal. You see, since my son is dead, Robert's mother, Lorraine Jennings, is now the person who would legally be entitled to his sole custody. I don't intend to let Lorraine bring up my grandson. I never did think it was a good idea.

"I want the legal custody of Robert. Lorraine doesn't like me. She doesn't want me to have much to do with Robert. She says she doesn't intend to have any child of hers brought up to be a financial robot. As it happens, Mr. Mason, while I have always tried to control my feelings, I am very, very fond of my grandson. There is where you can help me."

"How?" Mason asked.

"By proving Lorraine Jennings guilty of my son's murder," Horace Selkirk said, pushing back his chair. "In that way you acquit your client and at the same time make it possible for me to achieve my own goal. And if you need help in order to do it, you may call on me for anything you need. In the meantime, I'll be doing a few things on my own. Thank you, Mr. Mason, and good night."

He bowed formally and withdrew without shaking hands.

"Whew!" Della Street said. "There's a man who gives me the creeps."

Mason watched the banker's retreating figure. "There's a man," he said thoughtfully, "who can be very, very damned dangerous."

"And very, very damned disagreeable," Della Street said. "He's ruined a mighty good dinner."

Mason said thoughtfully, "He may do more than that. He may be going to ruin a mighty good case."

"Or save it," Della said.

"Or save it," Mason agreed dubiously and without even the faintest enthusiasm. "When a man like that starts messing around with the evidence, you can't tell *what* will happen."

9

∎

"WELL," DELLA STREET SAID, AS MASON SIGNED THE check at the restaurant, "what happens next? There was some talk about dancing, you'll remember."

Mason nodded, said, "First we're going to give Paul Drake a buzz and let him know where we are."

Della Street blew a kiss at the ceiling.

"Meaning?" Mason asked.

"Good-by dancing," Della said.

"Probably not," Mason said. "There's nothing much we can do tonight. Paul is holding the fort, but it's too soon for him to have any real reults. We'll call him just to keep him in good spirits. Give him a ring, Della, and ask him if there's anything particularly important."

Della Street went to the phone booth, dialed Paul Drake's number, and was back within less than a minute.

"He says we're to come up there right away," she said. "It's important—now don't ever say anything about a woman's intuition again, Mr. Perry Mason."

"Did he say what it was?"

"Lots of things," she said. "Among other things he has the name of the baby sitter."

"Oh-oh," Mason said. "That's a break. How did he get that?"

"He woudn't say. Says he's sitting on four telephone lines, all of them going like mad; that we're not to gum up his circuits by telephone calls, but that we'd better get up there."

Mason grinned. "Everybody seems to be ordering us around tonight, Della."

"Just restaurant managers, bankers and detectives, so far," she pointed out.

They drove to the office building, put his car in its accustomed parking space, took the elevator up to Drake's office.

The night switchboard operator, looking back over her shoulder, nodded to Mason and gestured down the corridor toward Drake's private office.

There were four lights glowing simultaneously on the switchboard.

Mason grinned at Della and said, "I guess the guy's busy. Come on, Della."

He opened the gate at the end of the enclosure which served as a reception room and Mason and Della Street walked down the long corridor past half-a-dozen different doors to enter Paul Drake's private office.

Drake looked up as they entered, nodded, said into the telephone, "Okay, stay with it. Now I want everything you can get on that . . . okay, call in just as soon as you get a chance."

Drake took a big bite from a hamburger sandwich, mumbled while he was chewing, "Sit down. I'm going to eat while I have a chance. These phones are driving me crazy."

He poured coffee into a big mug, put in cream and sugar, gulped a swallow of the coffee, said, "I can never get to eat a hamburger before it gets soggy."

"You wanted to see us?" Mason said.

"You've eaten?" Drake asked.

Mason nodded.

"I know," Drake said. "A thick filet mignon or a New York cut, French fried onions, imported red wine, baked potatoes with sour cream, coffee and apple pie a la mode—don't tell me, it's torture."

"Go ahead," Mason said, "torture yourself."

Drake regarded the soggy hamburger with distaste, started to take a bite but stopped as the telephone jangled.

Drake unerringly picked the one of the four telephones on which the call was coming in, held it to his ear, said, "Drake talking . . . okay . . . go on, give it to me."

Drake listened carefully, asked, "How do they know?" He listened some more, then said, "Okay, keep an ear to the ground. Hang around Headquarters. Keep in touch with the boys in the press room. They'll be looking for a late story."

Drake hung up the phone, picked up the remnants of the hamburger sandwich, looked at it for a moment, then with a gesture of disgust threw it into the waste-basket.

"What gives?" Mason asked.

"I ruined my appetite for that stuff talking about your nice meal," Drake said. "We have the name of the baby sitter, Perry."

"Who?"

"She's a professional. Works through an agency. It's called the Nite-Out Agency. That's spelled N-i-t-e—O-u-t. It specializes in baby sitters. Her name is Hannah Bass. I have a complete description with make of car, license number and everything here on a card for you."

Drake slid over a neatly typewritten card.

"How the devil did you get that?" Mason asked.

"Leg work," Paul Drake said wearily. "One time the Jennings' phone was out of order. They wanted a baby sitter. They went over to one of the neighbors, asked to use the phone, had forgotten the number of the agency. The phone book wasn't handy. They called Information and asked for the number of the Nite-Out Agency, and the woman who lived there in the house happened to remember the name Nite-Out because it struck her as such a nice name for a baby-sitting agency."

"Then you called up and asked for the name of the woman who did baby sitting for Jennings?" Della Street asked.

Drake shook his head. "You can't be that crude in this game. You might get slapped down. Moreover, they might tip off someone whom you didn't want tipped off.

"I played it the long way round. I had my man camp there with the neighbors and keep talking, asking them to try and remember any other conversation. They remembered that the baby sitter had been mentioned by name. They remembered the first name was Hannah because it was the name of their aunt, and they had been wondering whether their aunt might not have been making a little money on the side by baby sitting, so they perked their ears up. But it turned out the last name didn't mean anything to them so they forgot it. They thought the name was Fish. But then that didn't sound right. Then the man thought it might have been Trout. And then the woman remembered it was Bass. They'd taken one of those memory courses where they use association of ideas to help in recalling things. They could both of them remember Fish, but it was just luck they remembered Bass."

"That's the name all right?"

"That's the name all right," Drake said. "I telephoned the Nite-Out Agency and asked them if they had a Hannah Bass working for them and if they could recommend her credit. They said they didn't know anything about her financial affairs but she was one of their baby sitters; that she was very well liked; that they had never had any complaints; that they had investigated her character before taking her on as one of their sitters, and that she was thoroughly reliable and they had no hesitancy in recommending her for jobs. They felt under the circumstances her credit should be all right."

Again the telephone rang. Drake picked up one of the instruments, said, "Yeah? Hello. This is Paul Drake.

"The hell . . . you're sure . . . ? Okay. Keep me posted on anything new. Good-by."

Drake hung up the telephone, turned to Perry Mason and said, "That's a hell of a note. Someone has messed up the gun they found under the pillow where your client had been sleeping."

"What do you mean?" Mason asked.

"Someone ran a rattail file up and down the barrel until the thing is all scratched and cut. Test bullets fired through it are valueless."

"Then how can they tell it's the murder gun?" Mason asked.

Drake grinned. "That's the hell of it; they can't. You can imagine how Hamilton Burger, the district attorney, feels. He's biting his fingernails back to the knuckles."

Mason was thoughtful. "If that gun was found under Norda Allison's pillow it was planted there. She left that house early in the morning and went to a hotel. Do you think she'd have gone away and left a gun under the pillow?"

"Save it for the jury," Drake said, "don't try it on a detective with a bad stomach."

"What's the physical history of the gun?" Mason asked.

"It was purchased by Barton Jennings. He doesn't have a permit. He used it on a camping trip up in Idaho. He was hunting and said he wanted to take along a .22 to get some game."

"How does he explain its being under Norda Allison's pillow?"

"*He* doesn't explain. *He* doesn't have to."

"It was his gun," Mason said. "It should have been in his possession. It's up to him to explain. Where did he keep it?"

"In a bureau drawer in the room where they put Norda Allison for the night."

"And very conveniently left the gun in the drawer for her to find?"

"That's their story."

"That's a hell of a story," Mason said. "Anything else, Paul?"

"Yeah. I've got the names of the people who were with Mervin Selkirk up in San Francisco. That is, a newspaper reporter up there got them."

"Go on," Mason said.

"Well, Mervin Selkirk hit this fellow with brass knuckles. They've now established that as a fact. Some inoffensive bird named Benedict was the target. Selkirk had the brass knuckles and he was laying for Benedict. He socked the guy and then slipped the brass knuckles to this other chap who pretended he didn't want to have his name involved as a witness and got the hell out of there."

"You got the story?" Mason asked.

"I've got the story. So have the police. So have the newspapers."

"How did you get it?"

"I got it after the reporters dug out the facts. My San

Francisco correspondent knew I was working on the case. I was trying to get some angles up there and they called me as soon as it broke."

"What's the name of the fellow who went out with the brass knuckles?" Mason asked.

"Nick Fallon," Drake said. "His full name is Arturas Francisco Fallon, but Nick is a nickname. He's the guy who furnished the brass knuckles. Selkirk knew he had them; said he wanted to borrow them; had them in his pocket; stuck his foot out when Benedict walked by. Then when Benedict stumbled, he began cussing him and as Benedict straightened up to show a little indignation, Selkirk cracked him on the jaw, then slipped the knuckles back to Fallon—Fallon knew what he was supposed to do right quick. He got out of there fast."

Mason digested that information, turned to Della Street, said, "Okay, Della, let's go."

"Dancing?" she asked.

Mason shook his head. "Come on," he said.

"Where will you be?" Drake asked.

"We'll be in touch with you, Paul. Keep on the job. Get all the information you can. What have they done with Norda Allison?"

"They're booking her for suspicion of murder."

"Find out anything about Robert Selkirk, the seven-year-old son of Mervin by his former marriage?"

"Not yet," Drake said. "He's supposed to be on some kind of a camping trip. He and his dog went out with a Scout group of some sort. They're on a two- or three-day camping trip."

"I have a tip he's not with that group," Mason said.

"Then I've sure sent a man on a wild-goose chase," Drake told him. "He's rented a jeep and is going in over mountain roads. I told him to find out if Robert was with the group, then get to the nearest phone and let me know."

"When will you be hearing from him?"

"Probably within an hour."

"We'll call you back," Mason said. "Come on, Della."

They rode down in the elevator.

"How," Mason asked, "would you like to pose as my wife?"

Her eyes were without expression. "How long?" she asked tonelessly.

"An hour or two."

"What for?"

"We're going to borrow a baby."

"Oh, *are* we?"

"And then phone for a baby sitter," Mason said. "Know anybody in your apartment house who would co-operate?"

Della Street thought things over for a moment, then said, "Well . . . there's a grass widow on the lower floor . . . the baby'd be asleep."

"That's fine," Mason said. "We'll see if we can fix it up."

She laughed enigmatically, said, "I thought for a moment your intentions were . . . skip it."

Mason drove her to her apartment house, opened the door of the car. She jumped out on the other side. "Let's go."

They went up to Della's apartment. Della excused herself and a moment later came back with a woman of about her own age.

"This is Mrs. Colton, Mr. Mason. I've asked her if we could borrow her baby and . . . well, she wanted to look you over."

"We need a baby sitter," Mason said, "and I want it to look convincing. You can stay out in the hall if you want."

"Oh, I don't think that's necessary," she said, laughing. "I just wanted to size up the situation. It's such an unusual request."

"She's asleep now," Della Street explained, "but we can move her bed in here or we could put her in my bed."

76

"It's going to look rather crowded for a couple and a baby," Mason pointed out.

"You ought to see my apartment if you think this one would look crowded," Mrs. Colton said.

Della Street looked at Mason and raised her eyebrows. Mason nodded.

"Well, thanks a lot, Alice," Della said. "If you don't mind, we'll bring her in."

"Need help?" Mason asked.

"With the crib, yes," Mrs. Colton said. "I think we'd better bring her up in the crib. In that way we won't waken her—I hope."

Mason went to Mrs. Colton's apartment. The woman, Della Street and Mason carried the crib with the sleeping child to Della Street's apartment.

Mason seated himself, thumbed through the pages of the telephone book, got the number of the Nite-Out Agency and entered it in his notebook.

"You'd better call me if she wakens," Alice Colton said. "She knows you, Della, but if she should waken and find herself in a strange apartment, she . . . well, I'd like to be there."

"Don't worry," Della said. "We'll call you. We just want to use her for a short time for . . . look, Alice, why don't you stay right here with us?"

"Would it be all right if I did?"

"Sure it would," Della said. "Only just be careful to appear as a friend of ours and not as her mother. For the purposes of this masquerade I want to be the mother of the baby."

She turned toward Perry Mason and elevated her eyebrows.

Mason nodded, picked up the telephone, dialed the number of the agency.

"Hello," he said, when a voice answered. "We find ourselves confronted with an emergency. We need a baby sitter right away and it may be she will have to stay here all night. I'm not certain.

"Now we're willing to pay forty dollars for the right person, if she'll be willing to stay all night."

The voice of the woman at the agency was reassuring. "That will be *quite* satisfactory. I'm certain we can get you a reliable sitter for that price."

"Well now," Mason told her, "there's a problem. My wife is very nervous and we simply won't feel satisfied if we leave the child with someone who is a total stranger."

"Do you know any of our sitters?" the voice asked.

"Not personally," Mason said, "but you have a Hannah Bass. Some people who have used your agency recommend her very highly. Would it be possible for you to get her?"

"I'll see," the voice said. "If you'll give me your telephone number, I'll find out and call you back."

Mason gave her the number and hung up.

Alice Colton watched them with puzzled eyes.

"It's all right, Alice," Della Street said.

A few moments later Della Street's telephone rang. Mason answered it.

"This is the Nite-Out Agency," the feminine voice said. "We've contacted Hannah Bass and it's quite all right with her. She wants to know, however, if it is definitely assured that it will be an all-night job and that you are willing to pay forty dollars."

"That's right," Mason said. "If anything happens and the emergency doesn't materialize, she'll get the forty dollars anyway and cab fare home."

"She has her own car. Will you give me your name and address?"

"The apartment," Mason said, "is in my wife's name. I'm a buyer for a large concern and I don't want to be disturbed on week ends by a lot of salesmen who are trying to interest me in bargains. The name is Della Street. You have the telephone number and if you have a pencil, I'll give you the address."

Mason gave her the address of Della Street's apartment house and the feminine voice said, "Mrs. Bass will be there within thirty minutes."

"Thank you," Mason said.

"Is it a job where she can get some sleep, or will she have to sit up?" the feminine voice inquired.

"She'll have to sit up and watch the baby," Mason said. "I'm sorry but that's the way it is."

"That's quite all right. She's prepared to do that. She'll stay until eight in the morning, or nine if necessary."

"Have her come right along, if you will, please," Mason said.

He hung up the telephone.

Alice Colton looked around the apartment, said, "The feminine influence predominates pretty much, Della. Mr. Mason doesn't seem to be . . . well, he doesn't seem to *live* here."

Mason said, "I guess you have a point there. If you folks will pardon me."

He took off his coat, untied his necktie, opened the shirt at the neck, kicked off his shoes, settled back in his stocking feet, picked up the paper and turned to the sporting section.

"How's that?" he asked.

"Better," Alice Colton said smiling. "You know, you two . . . well, when you look like that you . . . you seem to sort of fit in."

"Thanks," Mason said as Della Street blushed slightly.

Alice Colton continued to regard them with speculative curiosity.

"Now when Mrs. Bass comes in," Mason said to Alice Colton, "we're going to have to have a story for her. It's this: Della and I are married. You're Della's sister. Your mother is very ill and we're trying to get a plane to Denver.

"My sister is coming in tomorrow to relieve the baby sitter and take care of the child until we return. We're awaiting confirmation on plane tickets.

"Della, you'd better load up a couple of suitcases and

79

bring them out here and you, Mrs. Colton, had better get a suitcase and have it ready.

"And while you're about it, Mrs. Colton, I'd appreciate it if you'd ring up Western Union and send a telegram to Della Street at this address saying: Mother passed away an hour ago. No need to make the trip. Will advise you concerning funeral arrangements. Florence."

"You want that sent?"

"I want it sent," Mason said. "Go to your apartment and get a suitcase, throw some books in it or anything you want and come back here, but telephone that message just before you leave your apartment. You'll have to charge it to your phone. Della will fix up the financial arrangements."

"This is a real thrill," Mrs. Colton said, laughing nervously. "I feel all cloak-and-daggerish."

"This is routine," Della Street said, laughing.

"After Mrs. Bass comes," Mason instructed Mrs. Colton, "you're to be the tragic one. Della and I will take it more or less as a matter of course. Della will be philosophical about her mother. After all, she's been sick and the end was not unexpected. You will be quiet and moody and perhaps sob a bit in a quiet, unobtrusive way—you will however, listen very carefully to everything that is said and remember what is said because you may have to testify."

"In court?" Alice Colton asked in consternation.

"Sure," Mason said, making his voice sound casual. "There's nothing to it. Just get up on the witness stand and tell what you heard. Della Street will be right along with you. Just be sure you're telling the truth and there's nothing to worry about."

Alice Colton laughed nervously. "Good heavens," she said, "I'll never sleep tonight, not a wink. I'll get the suitcase and send the telegram."

She was back in some ten minutes carrying a suitcase. In the meantime Della Street had placed two suitcases near the door.

A few minutes later the street bell rang and Hannah Bass announced herself.

"Come on up," Della Street said. "My husband is just dressing but he's decent. We're awaiting a wire from Denver and a confirmation of plane reservations. If you can come right up, we'll explain your duties."

A few moments later chimes sounded and Della Street opened the door.

Hannah Bass was in the middle forties, a matronly appearing, muscular woman whose body appeared thick rather than fat. Her eyes were small, restless and glittering.

Della Street came toward her, said, "I'm Mrs. Street and this is my husband. This is my sister. We're waiting for a confirmation of reservations."

Mason, who had been adjusting his tie in front of the mirror, smiled and said, "Do sit down, Mrs. Bass. The baby is in the bedroom. I'm quite certain you won't have any trouble. My sister will be here by morning. You see, my mother-in-law is quite ill."

Hannah Bass shook hands with the others, sat down on the edge of the davenport, gray restless eyes surveying the apartment, taking in every detail. "How old's the baby?" she asked.

"My daughter is sixteen months old," Della Street said. "You won't have any trouble, I'm certain."

"Sometimes when a baby wakes up with a stranger," Mrs. Bass said, "she gets panic stricken and . . ."

"Not Darlene," Della Street interrupted. "I can guarantee she won't give you any trouble. She's a lamb. Just tell her that Mommie asked you to wait until Aunt Helen could come. Tell her that Aunt Helen will be here in the morning."

"You don't think you should wake her up now and tell her that you have to go?"

"Oh, we've already told her," Della Street said. "We told her that Mommie was going to have to go away and that a friend of Mommie's would stay with her until Aunt

Helen came. She'll wake about seven in the morning, and I'm certain you won't have any trouble. Helen will be here by seven-thirty or eight."

Hannah Bass seemed a little dubious. "Sometimes they get frightened," she said.

"I know," Della Street said, "but this is an emergency."

"After all," Mason said reassuringly, "we *may* not have to go. If we can't get confirmation of our reservations on this plane, we just can't make it and that's all there is to it."

Hannah Bass looked at him coldly. "I understood it was a forty-dollar job," she said.

"It is," Mason told her. "You get the same amount of money whether we go or whether we don't. Just sit back and relax."

Alice Colton wiped her eyes with a handkerchief.

Della Street said, "It's all right, Alice. Everything's going to be for the best."

"The agency tells me that you asked especially for me."

Della Street looked inquiringly at Perry Mason.

Mason said, "That's right, Mrs. Bass. You see, I'd heard about you through the Jennings. They speak very highly of you."

"The Jennings?" she asked.

"Lorraine and Barton Jennings," Mason explained. They have a boy, Robert Selkirk. Her child by another marriage."

"Oh, yes," she said. "Bobby is quite a boy. He has a certain dignity that is exceptional in a child."

"Crazy about guns, isn't he?" Mason said.

"Well, he's like any normal boy—what can you expect with all these 'pistol pictures' on television. He loves to watch galloping horses and, after all, those shows put on some pretty spirited gun battles."

"They do for a fact," Mason agreed. And then added, "I suppose Robert has his special pearl-handled imitation six-shooters with the holsters tied down in the most approved Western style."

Hannah Bass became suddenly uneasy. "He likes guns," she said, and clamped her lips together.

Mason eyed her thoughtfully. "That," he said, "is the only thing which caused us some uneasiness, Mrs. Bass."

"What is?" she asked, instantly on the defensive.

"Giving Robert a real gun to play with."

"Who says I gave him a real gun?"

Mason let his face show surprise. "Didn't you?"

"Who said so?"

"Why I understood that you did. Barton Jennings has this .22 automatic, you know, and Robert plays with it."

There was a long interval of silence. Hannah Bass had little suspicious gray eyes and they glittered as they probed Mason's face.

The lawyer met her gaze with searching candor. "Don't you let him play with Barton's gun?" he asked.

"What difference does it make?" Hannah Bass asked.

"I just wondered," Mason said.

"I don't talk about my other clients when I'm baby-sitting," Hannah Bass announced with finality.

Mason said deprecatingly, "We were only discussing your recommendations and the reason we sent for you, Mrs. Bass."

"I didn't know anybody knew about it," she said suddenly. "It was just a secret between Robert and me."

Mason's smile was enigmatic.

The street bell rang. Della Street went to the telephone, said, "Yes . . . oh, hurry up with it, will you? I'll open the door for you."

She pressed a buzzer and said to Perry Mason, "A Western Union telegram."

Mason showed excitement. "He's on the way up?"

Della nodded.

Alice Colton said, "Oh, Della," and suddenly flung herself into Della Street's arms.

Hannah Bass's glittering eyes kept moving around the

apartment, taking in every detail. "I want to look at the baby," she said suddenly.

Della Street glanced at Mason.

Mason partially opened the door of the bedroom.

Della Street continued to comfort Alice Colton.

Hannah Bass got up and strode to the bedroom door, looked inside at the sleeping child, then stepped inside the bedroom and looked around.

The buzzer sounded on the door of Della Street's apartment.

Della Street disengaged herself from Alice and went to the door. She accepted the telegram, signed for it and tore the envelope open.

For a moment she stood there with the telegram in her hand saying nothing.

"Oh, Della, it isn't . . . it isn't . . . ?"

Della Street nodded, said, "Mother has passed away."

There was a long moment of silence, then Alice Colton began to sob audibly.

"Well, after all," Della Street said, "it's for the best. Mother was bedridden and she had nothing to look forward to. The doctors said there was virtually no hope."

Hannah Bass stood in the door of the bedroom for a moment. Then she marched over to where Della Street was holding the telegram, said, "Say, what kind of a plant *is* this, anyway?"

"What do you mean?" Della Street asked.

"You know what I mean," Hannah said, snatching at Della Street's left hand. Where's your wedding ring?"

"At the jewelers, being repaired," Della Street said coldly. "That is, if it's any of *your* business."

"It's lots of my business," Hannah Bass said. "You're not married. That's not your baby. This isn't your husband. I've seen his face somewhere before—in newspapers and magazines somewhere—what are you trying to do?"

Della Street said, "My mother has just passed away. Here's the telegram."

She extended the telegram, holding her thumb over the top part of the telegram so that Hannah Bass could see the message, but not the place where the telegram had originated.

"Well, we won't argue about it," the woman said. "This was a forty-dollar job. Give me my forty dollars and I'll be on my way."

Della Street looked at Perry Mason.

Mason smiled and shook his head.

"Now don't pull that line with me," Hannah Bass said belligerently.

"What line?" Mason asked.

"Trying to talk me out of the forty dollars."

"No one's trying to talk you out of the forty dollars, Mrs. Bass," Mason told her. "What you wanted, you know, was an all-night job; you wanted to be guaranteed it would be an all-night job. It is."

"I wanted the forty dollars, not necessarily an all-night job."

"You'll get the forty dollars," Mason told her, "and you'll sit right there all night to earn it."

Hannah Bass looked at him sharply. "You're the lawyer," she said. "You're the man who does all that spectacular stuff in court. You're Perry Mason!"

"That's right," Mason said. "Now, then, just sit down there and tell me how it happened that you would let Robert Selkirk play with a real gun whenever you were baby-sitting with him."

"So *that's* what you're after!" Hannah Bass said.

"That's what I'm after," Mason told her.

Hannah Bass slowly seated herself. "So this was all a plant."

"It was all a plant, if that will make you feel any better," Mason told her.

"I don't have to answer your questions. I can get up and walk out through that door. You don't have any authority to question me."

"That's entirely correct," Mason said. "You were hired

to sit here until eight o'clock in the morning. You're to get forty dollars for it. If you walk out through that door, you don't get the forty dollars and you'll still have to answer the same questions; but this time before a grand jury."

"What difference does it make?" Hannah Bass asked.

"For your information, so there won't be any misunderstanding, Mervin Selkirk was murdered. Norda Allison has been accused of that murder. She's my client.

"I don't know what happened. I'm trying to find out. I'm not making any accusations, at least not yet, but apparently when you were baby-sitting you let Robert have a .22 automatic, probably a Colt Woodsman model."

"You can't prove it," Hannah Bass said.

"I think I can," Mason told her. "If you have anything to conceal, if you are implicated in any way in the murder of Mervin Selkirk, you had better get out of here and retain a lawyer to represent you. If you have nothing to conceal, there is no reason why you can't talk to me."

"You got me here under false pretenses," she said.

"I asked you to come here," Mason told her. "I wanted to talk with you where I wouldn't be interrupted by the police."

"What do you mean, the police?"

"*You* should know what I mean. The police are employed by the taxpayers to look into matters of this sort. In case you haven't met Lieutenant Tragg of the homicide department, you have a delightful experience in store. Tragg is very thorough, very shrewd, very fair and very determined.

"Sooner or later you're going to have to tell your story —officially. You can tell it to me now unofficially. If there's anything about it that sounds fishy, I'll point it out."

"Why should any of it sound fishy?" she asked.

"I don't know," Mason said. "All I know is that your extreme reluctance to talk may be an indication of guilty knowledge. You'd better consult a lawyer, if that's the case.

"And remember this, Mrs. Bass, someday you're going to be on the witness stand and I'm going to cross-examine you and if you don't tell me your story now, I'm going to ask you why you were afraid to tell it."

"Who says I'm afraid to tell it?"

"I say so."

"Well I'm not."

"Then why won't you tell it?"

"I didn't say I wouldn't tell it."

"Make up your mind."

The room was silent for several seconds, then Hannah Bass said, "There wasn't anything wrong with it, it was just yielding to a childish whim. Robert is an unusual boy. He loves Western pictures. He wants to grow up and be a marshal or a cowpuncher or something of that sort. He's crazy about firearms. I've never seen anything like it."

"How did it happen that you started letting him have the .22?" Mason asked.

"It was one time when I was baby-sitting with him. I had to stay there for two days while Mr. and Mrs. Jennings were away. They left Robert with me."

"You occupied the spare bedroom on the second floor?"

"Yes."

"At the front of the house?"

"Yes."

"Go on," Mason said.

"Well, I opened a drawer in the bureau in order to put some of my things away and found this gun."

"What sort of a gun?"

"A Colt Woodsman."

"You know something about guns?"

"I was married to a man who ran shooting galleries. He was one of the best shots in the country. He taught me how to handle guns."

"And how to shoot?" Mason asked.

"I became a very good shot," she admitted.

"All right, what happened?"

"Robert came walking into the room while I was looking this gun over. He was completely fascinated with it. He wanted to hold it for a while."

"What did you do?"

"I took out the magazine clip and saw that it was fully loaded. I snapped back the recoil-operated mechanism and found there was no shell in the barrel. So I let Robert handle the gun."

"And then what happened?"

"He was completely fascinated. He had seen me work the mechanism. He wanted to know how to handle the gun and all about it.

"So then I took the shells out of the magazine, put the magazine in place and let him play with the empty gun for a while. Then I put it back in the drawer. I don't think Robert talked about anything else all day. I was afraid his parents wouldn't like what I had done, although for my part I think the best way to teach boys about firearms is to teach them at an early age and teach them to handle them safely. However, all parents don't have the same idea."

"So what did you do?" Mason asked.

"I made Robert promise that he wouldn't tell his folks anything about that gun."

"And after that?" Mason asked.

"Well," she said, somewhat reluctantly, "after that Robert had sort of a hold on me. When his parents would be gone he'd insist on having me unload the gun and let him keep it in his hand. At first I made him stay in the house, but after a while—well, I let him take it outdoors and play with it.

"For the life of me I don't see that there was anything wrong with what I did, but there were times when I felt as though I should go to Mrs. Jennings and discuss the matter with her.

"The trouble was I had already let Robert play with the weapon. I don't think I have ever seen a child as completely fascinated with any toy as Robert was with just holding that automatic in his hands."

"Did he ever pull the trigger?" Mason asked.

"Of course he did. However, I made him promise that he'd never, never pull the trigger when the gun was pointed at anyone. I showed him the safety, showed him how to put it on and keep it on, and it was part of his agreement with me that he was always to have this safety in place while he was handling the gun."

"You were there with him at night?" Mason asked.

"Sometimes. I've stayed as much as a couple of days at a time."

"And Robert has played with the gun each time?"

"Yes."

"And at night has he ever slept with the gun under his pillow?"

"Once, yes."

"How did that happen?"

"He's a rather nervous, high-strung child despite the fact that he keeps his emotions under such excellent control. He liked to camp out in that tent on the patio and he told me it would give him a feeling of assurance if he had the gun with him. He said there were noises in the night and he wanted some protection, was the way he expressed it."

"And you let him take the gun?"

"Just that once. That was when I found he had a shell for it. That's when I began to get frightened of the whole business. I told him he was just a little boy seven years old, that he couldn't have any gun for protection until he got to be a big man."

"Now then, when Lorraine Jennings and Barton Jennings went down on Friday night to meet Norda Allison at the airport, did you take care of Robert?"

She shook her head.

"Who did?"

"I think they left him there alone with the dog. Rover wouldn't let anyone get near Robert. I think his folks put Robert to bed and then just quietly went down to meet the plane."

"Would they leave him alone like that?"

"Sometimes. The dog was always there. Sometimes they'd leave after he'd gone to sleep. I don't like the idea of that. I think that whenever you are planning on leaving a child alone, you should tell him. I think if a child wakes up at night and finds he's alone, when he expects his parents to be there, it gives him an emotional shock."

"Did they ever say anything to you at any time about the gun, or did you ever say anything to them? In other words, do you think that they knew you were letting him take the gun?"

"I never said anything to them and they never said anything to me. Robert promised me that he wouldn't tell them and I'm satisfied he wouldn't. Robert is a child, but he's a man of his word."

"But you do know Robert wanted the gun when he was sleeping out in the patio?"

"Yes."

"If Robert had wakened and wanted something in the house and had found his mother and his stepfather were away, do you think it is possible that he could have gone to that bedroom and taken the gun out of the drawer?"

A look of sudden alarm came on her face.

"Do you?" Mason asked.

"Good heavens, *did* he do that?" she asked in a half whisper.

"I'm asking you if it's possible."

"It's very possible," she said.

Mason smiled and said, "I think that does it, Mrs. Bass. Here's your forty dollars for the baby-sitting."

"Good heavens," she said, "if he had done that, if Mr. Mason, do you think that child could possibly have . . . good heavens, no! It's preposterous! He wouldn't have done anything like that!"

Mason said, "Those are the words you use to reassure yourself, Mrs. Bass, but if there had been a mirror

90

in front of your face, you would have seen from your dismayed expression exactly how possible you thought that would have been."

Mason handed her four ten-dollar bills.

Hannah Bass blinked for a moment, then abruptly got up and without a word walked out into the corridor, pulling the door shut behind her.

Mason smiled reassuringly at Alice Colton. "You may take the child back now, Mrs. Colton, and thanks a lot. We certainly appreciate your co-operation. You may have aided the cause of justice."

10

IT WAS TEN O'CLOCK ON SUNDAY MORNING WHEN MAson's unlisted telephone rang.

Mason picked up the receiver. "This is Perry."

Paul Drake's voice, sharp with urgency, came over the telephone. "I have something, Perry, that you'd better look into. I'm afraid my man pulled a boner, but there was nothing to tip him off."

"What do you mean by that?"

"I had tails put on the Jennings' house the way you wanted. Barton Jennings went out this morning, visited an apartment house and then came back. My man tailed him both ways, but he's a little uneasy about it."

"Why?" Mason asked.

"Call it an investigator's sixth sense, if you want," Drake said, "but my man feels that Barton Jennings went out there on a specific errand and managed to accomplish that errand right under the nose of the operative."

"Where's your man now?"

"Up here."

"You're at the office?"

"Yes."

"Hold him there," Mason said. "I'm coming up."

Mason telephoned the garage man in the apartment house to have his car ready for action. He took the elevator to the garage, jumped in his car, drove to the all but deserted parking lot in front of the office building, left his car and went to Drake's office.

Drake's operative was a small man whose silvery-gray eyes were thoughtfully watchful beneath bushy white eyebrows. He was small in stature, somewhere in his late fifties, and as keenly incisive as a sharp razor. He had, nevertheless, cultivated a habit of blending into the background as successfully as a chameleon.

Mason had a vague impression that this man's name was Smith. He had met him on half a dozen different cases but had never heard him referred to by any other name than "Smithy."

Paul Drake, tilted back in his chair with his heels up on the desk, smoking a contemplative cigarette, waved a greeting to Mason.

Smithy shook hands.

Mason sat down.

"You tell him, Smithy," Drake said.

The operative said, "At eight o'clock this morning Barton Jennings left his house carrying a suitcase. He was moving with some difficulty. His leg was bothering him. He had a cane in one hand, the suitcase in the other. He got in his automobile and drove very slowly and casually down to a gas station. He had the car filled up with gas, the windshield washed, the tires checked, then he drove around the block and started back toward home.

"Just something about the way the fellow was driving the car made me feel he had something in mind that he intended to do, if he was certain he wasn't wearing a tail. So I hung way, way back, just taking a chance.

"Then I saw him swing over to the side of the road a bit. I've had guys pull that trick on me before, so I turned down a side street, went for half a block and made a U turn.

"Sure enough, Jennings did just what I thought he was going to do. He made a complete U turn and came tearing back down the street going fast. I was where I could get a brief glimpse of the maneuver, so I came dawdling out of the side street at slow speed and crossed the intersection just ahead of him. That gave him a chance to pass me and it never occurred to him I was following him. After about eight or ten blocks at high speed he slowed down and then drove directly to this apartment house.

"He parked the car, took the suitcase, went in, and was there for about half an hour; then he came out and drove to his house. After he left the apartment house, he didn't take any precautions to see that he was free of a tail. He had all the assurance of a man who had accomplished a mission and wasn't worrying about anything any more. He had the same suitcase with him that he'd taken in."

"He went home?" Mason asked.

"He went home, put his car in the garage, went in the house, and after a while came out and sat on the porch, ostensibly reading the Sunday papers, but actually looking around to see if anybody was keeping him under surveillance.

"When a subject does that, it's a lot better to get off the job and have somebody else come on, so I beat it to a phone, telephoned Paul for a relief and told him I had something to report."

"You have any idea what apartment the guy went to?" Mason asked.

"No."

"What apartment house was it?"

"The Cretonic. It's a small apartment house out on Wimberly. I don't think there are over fifteen or twenty apartments in the place altogether. It's a walk-up, two-story affair, moderately priced apartments—the kind that would appeal to persons in the low white-collar brackets."

"Let's go," Mason said.

"I thought you'd want to take a look," Smithy said. "Two cars?"

"One," Mason said. "We'll go in mine. You sit here on the job, Paul, and we may telephone for some help. Come on, Smithy, let's go."

Smithy and the lawyer took the elevator down to Mason's car, drove out to the Cretonic apartments. Mason got out and looked the place over.

"Jennings needed a key," Mason said, "to get in or else he pressed the bell of some apartment and they buzzed the door open."

Smithy nodded.

"You don't have any idea which?"

"No, Mr. Mason, I don't. I just wasn't close enough to see what he was doing, and I didn't dare to get close enough. I can tell you one thing though, he was stooped over here at the side of the building. I could see his left elbow hanging pretty well down."

"Well, that's a clue," Mason said. "Let's look at the lower cards."

Mason took his notebook, jotted down some names, said, "There's half a dozen, but that's still too many."

"I'll tell you what, Mr. Mason," Smithy said, "if you'll stand right here in the doorway and look down at the names on the directory and let your left arm stick out a little bit the way it would if you were leaning over and punching a button with your right thumb, I might be able to do a better job. I'll go back to the same place where I had my car parked and in that way we may be able to narrow it down a little bit."

"Go ahead," Mason told him.

He waited until the detective was in the right position and then Mason stooped down and made a pretense of jabbing each one of the lower call buttons with his thumb.

When he had finished, Smithy came moving up and

said, "I think it's the lowest one on the left-hand side, Mr. Mason. Your elbow looked just about right then."

Mason examined the card. It was oblong, but evidently from an engraved calling card, and said simply, *Miss Grace Hallum*.

"We'll give it a try," Mason said.

"Any idea what you're going to tell her?"

"I'm not going to tell her anything," Mason said. "She's going to tell us."

He pressed the button.

There was no answer.

Mason pressed the button two or three times more, then pressed the button marked *Manager*.

A moment later the outer lock buzzed open and Mason entered the small lobby. A door opened behind a counter in the corner of the lobby and an intelligent looking, well-kept woman in her early fifties stepped out to smile at the lawyer and the detective.

"Something for you gentlemen?" she asked.

"Vacancies?" Mason asked.

She smiled and shook her head.

"I understood that Grace Hallum's apartment was to be vacant," Mason said. "I tried to ring her but she doesn't answer. Do you know anything about her?"

"Oh yes," the manager said. "She's going to be gone for some little time. She made arrangements with me to feed her canary."

"When did she leave?" Mason asked.

The manager looked at him curiously. "Are you a detective?" she asked.

Mason grinned and jerked his thumb at Smithy. "He is."

"Oh—what's the trouble?"

"No trouble," Mason said. "We're just trying to get a line on her."

The manager's lips clamped together. "Well, I'm sorry. There's nothing I can tell you except that she's gone."

Mason played a hunch. "Did she have the boy with her?"

"She had the boy with her."

"Suitcases?"

"One doesn't go for an indefinite stay without suitcases."

"Taxicab?" Mason asked.

"I don't know. I didn't ask."

"Does she own a car?"

"I don't think so."

Mason tried to be as charming as possible. "It wouldn't hurt you to be a little more communicative."

"I'm not so certain about that. I don't discuss tenants' affairs."

"Oh well," Mason said, "it isn't particularly important. We're just checking, that's all. How long has she had the boy, do you know?"

"I'm sure I couldn't tell you."

"Well, thanks a lot," Mason said. "Good-by."

He gave her his best smile and led the way out of the apartment house.

"I don't get it," Smithy said.

"What?"

"Your technique," Smithy told him. "I'd have flashed my credentials and suggested she might get into trouble if she tried to withhold information."

"I have a better idea," Mason told him, studying the directory. "Let's see, Grace Hallum was in 208. Let's look at 206 and 210—who's in 206?"

Smithy consulted the directory.

"Miss M. Adrian," he said.

"Give her a ring," Mason instructed.

Smithy pressed his thumb against the button.

In a few moments the door was buzzed open.

Mason and the detective again entered the apartment house. The manager had now retreated into her apartment and the door behind the little counter was closed.

The two men climbed the steps to the second floor.

Mason tapped on the door of 206.

The door opened the scant two or three inches allowed by a heavy brass safety chain. A woman with a long, thin nose surveyed the two men suspiciously. "What is it?" she asked.

Mason studied the blinking eyes, the nose, the thin lips, the prominent chin, said, "Show her your credentials, Smithy."

Smithy took a worn billfold from his pocket, extended it so the woman could look it over.

"Detectives!" she said.

"Smithy is a detective," Mason said. "I'm a lawyer. We want to talk with you."

"What's *your* name?"

Mason gave her his card.

Her face showed surprise. She looked from the card to Mason's face and then said, "Good heavens, you *are!* Why *you're* Perry Mason."

"That's right."

The chain snapped off the catch. "Well, come in," she said. "I'm honored. Of course, I haven't been preparing for visitors and Sunday is usually my morning to straighten up the apartment. I usually go out to a movie on Saturday night and . . . well, sit down and tell me what this is all about."

"It's about your neighbor next door," Mason said.

Miss Adrian, a woman in her late fifties, small boned, spry as a bird, paused in mid-stride. "Well now, I just *knew* there was something wrong there," she said.

Mason nodded. "That's why we came to see you."

"But I didn't tell anybody. I've kept my own counsel. Now, how in the world did you know that I'd seen anything?"

"We have ways of finding out things like that," Mason said. "Would you mind telling us about it?"

"What do you want to know?"

"When did the boy come here?"

"Yesterday morning," she said. "Yesterday morning at exactly four-thirty-five."

"Do you know who brought him?"

"His father, I suppose."

"And what do you know about Grace Hallum?"

"She's divorced—lives on alimony. She works as a baby sitter part of the time for extra money and calls herself Miss Grace Hallum rather than Mrs. Hallum. She used to be a model and she never lets a body forget it."

"Does she work for the Nite-Out Agency?"

"I believe that's right, yes."

"Well, then," Mason said, smiling casually, "you didn't think there was anything unusual about it, simply someone bringing a boy to stay with her."

"Nothing unusual about it!" Miss Adrian exclaimed. "Well I *like* that!"

"There was something unusual then?"

"I'll say there was. At that hour in the morning with my wall bed down, my head right up against that partition and . . . I'll say one thing about this apartment house, the only way you can have any complete privacy is to talk in sign language."

"You heard what was said?"

"I heard enough of it."

"Such as what?"

"Well, Grace Hallum was a little shocked at the idea of being called at that hour in the morning but the man was a regular client of hers so she opened the door and let him in. Well, you know, she was terribly coy about not being dressed and all that."

"How old is she?"

"Twenty-seven, but she *says* it's twenty-four," Miss Adrian snapped, "and she has looks. She is very, very well aware of those looks and she had just as soon other people would be aware of them too, if you know what I mean. She's a blue-eyed, tall blonde and she's always posing. She wears dresses that show her hips, if you know what I mean."

"We know what you mean," Mason said affably. "Just what was the conversation?"

"This man wanted her to keep the boy until he gave her further instructions. He asked her to get some suitcases ready because she might have to travel and . . . that's about all there was to it yesterday morning."

"And then what happened after that?"

"Well, the man came up *this* morning and I've never heard such a conversation in my life."

"What do you mean?"

"The man was talking with the boy about some sort of a shooting. He kept saying, 'Now remember, *you* didn't shoot anyone. You had a bad dream,' and I heard the boy say, 'I did too shoot the pistol,' and the man laughed and said, 'So what of it?' and then said, 'You *thought* you shot the pistol, you dreamed you did, but the pistol really wasn't fired at all!' "

"Then what?"

"Then the boy said, 'No, I fired the pistol. The rest of it may have been a dream, but I know I fired the pistol.' "

"Go on," Mason said. "What happened after that?"

"Well, the man talked with the boy a while and said he was going to send him on a long trip with Miss Hallum and to be sure and be a good boy and do everything Miss Hallum told him to."

"Did Miss Hallum seem surprised?"

"Not her—now I can tell you this much, there's been a lot of goings on in that apartment, suitcases banging around, people coming with this and that. She was packing and talking with the boy and the boy was doing quite a bit of crying. He seemed to be terribly upset about something."

"Go on," Mason said.

"Well, that's about all I know except that another woman came and called on her last night. I gathered she was the woman who runs the Nite-Out Agency. They had quite a conversation. A lot of it was in whispers. Apparently the boy was asleep and they were trying to keep him from knowing anything about it."

"What happened this morning?" Mason asked.

"Well, this man came again with some clothes for the boy. Right after the man left she went to the phone and called a taxicab. I heard her say she wanted to go to the airport."

"The cab came?"

"That's right."

"And she left?"

"Yes, she and the boy."

"How long ago?"

"Well, it must have been—oh I guess an hour and a half ago."

"Did you have any idea where they were going?" Mason asked.

"The man said something about Mexico."

Mason got up and gave his hand to Miss Adrian. "Thank you very much for your co-operation," he said. "We're just checking."

"Well, for heaven's sake, I'll certainly say you're checking, coming around to see a body on a Sunday morning. Can you tell me what it's all about?"

"I'm sorry," Mason said. "We just wanted to make sure that the boy had left."

"Yes, he left all right, but can you tell me why all this mystery?"

Mason smiled and shook his head. "I'm terribly sorry, Miss Adrian, I hate to be a one-way street on these things, but you know how it is."

She sniffed, "Well, I can't say as I do. It seems to me that if *I* give *you* information, *you* should give *me* information."

"I may be back after a while," Mason said. "It may be a few hours or it may be a few days, but I'll talk with you some more and by that time I may be able to give you a little more information."

"Well, I'd certainly like to know what it's all about,"

she said. "It's not that I'm curious, you understand. I like to lead my own life and let other people lead theirs, but what's all this about a boy crying because he thinks he's fired a gun that his daddy didn't want him to, and all of that?"

"Oh, children do have nightmares," Mason said.

"Yes," she snapped. "Nightmares of shooting people and then they're brought to a baby sitter at half-past-four on a Saturday morning and then a lawyer and a detective come and ask questions. Don't think I'm foolish, Mr. Mason. I wasn't born yesterday."

Mason shook hands with her, held her hand for a long moment in his, patted the back of it with his left hand and said, "Now, don't go making a mountain out of a molehill, Miss Adrian, and please don't say anything to anybody else, at least for a while. I'd like to have the information all to myself for a day or so."

"And then you'll tell me what it's all about?"

Mason lowered his voice and said, "Look, if you'll be co-operative, I think I can promise you that you'll have an opportunity to get on the witness stand and—"

"The witness stand!" she almost screamed in dismay.

"That's right," Mason said, "you'll pose for newspaper photographs and your testimony may make quite a commotion. But that will only happen if you're very, very careful not to say anything to anyone prior to the time of trial."

"Good heavens, I don't *want* to get on the witness stand."

"Why not?"

"Standing up in front of all those people and telling how old I am."

Mason shook his head, "You won't have to tell how old you are, just say that you're over thirty. . . ." He paused to lean forward and look at her intently. "You *are* over thirty, aren't you?"

Miss Adrian was suddenly coy.

"Well," she said, "it's all right if someone doesn't ask

me how *much* over thirty I am . . . it's longer than I like to think of."

"That's all right," Mason said, "the judge will protect you. You won't have to tell anything about your age. Now, we've got to move on, Miss Adrian, but if you'll just try to think over the events of the last day or so —just so someone doesn't get you mixed up on cross-examination."

"Cross-examination?"

"Of course," Mason said casually, "all witnesses have to be cross-examined, but that's nothing."

"Well, I'd always heard it was quite an ordeal."

"Not if you're telling the truth."

"I'm telling the truth."

"And not if you remember *all* the details and don't get confused."

"Well, I remember all the details, but I don't know whether I'm going to get confused standing up there in front of a whole crowd of people like that."

Mason smiled affably. "Just start planning on what you're going to wear, Miss Adrian. I'm sure you'll want to look your best. Sometimes the flashlight photographs they use in newspapers aren't the most flattering photographs a person can have but . . . you'll be all right."

"Well, I'm glad you gave me some notice in advance," she said, going over to the mirror, patting her hair and smoothing the wave around back of the ears. "I'll tell the world some of those newspaper pictures *are* terrible!"

"Good-by," Mason said. "Remember now, not a word of this to anyone."

Mason let himself and the detective out in the corridor.

"Pay dirt," Smithy said under his breath.

"Pay dirt," Mason agreed. "Now we've got to phone Paul and get some operatives out at the airport in a rush."

11

FROM THE NEAREST PHONE MASON CALLED PAUL DRAKE.

"Rush some men out to the airport, Paul. Look for Robert Selkirk, a boy of seven years of age, aristocratic in bearing. He's accompanied by a woman named Grace Hallum, blonde, blue eyes, twenty-seven years old, with a good figure. She worked for a while as a model, married, collected some alimony and is living now partially on alimony and partially by supplementing her income by baby-sitting. They'll probably have a couple of hours' start on you and will have been on a plane for someplace outside of the jurisdiction of the local courts. Try Mexico City first, then try everything you can get. Cover all passenger lists, see if you can locate a woman, any woman, traveling with a seven-year-old boy."

"There'll be hundreds of them," Drake said.

"Not with a departure time of the last two hours. My best guess is that reservations were first made over the telephone, then Barton Jennings took some cash and some of the kid's clothes in a suitcase up to Grace Hallum's apartment. He transferred the clothes there, came out with the empty suitcase.

"A taxicab went to the Cretonic Apartments and picked them up. See if you can locate the cab driver, find out what airline they were traveling on. Get busy."

"Okay," Drake promised. "You coming up here?"

"We're on our way," Mason told him.

The lawyer hung up the phone and he and Smithy drove back to the parking place at the office.

"I could tell by the way he was carrying that suitcase when he came out that there was something wrong,"

Smith said. "That's what it was, all right; the suitcase was empty when he came out."

Mason nodded.

They entered the elevator.

"Your secretary just came in," the operator told Mason.

"Stop at Paul's office?" Mason asked.

"I don't think so. I think she went on down the corridor to your office."

"I'll pick her up," Mason said.

They stopped at Drake's office. "Go on in," Mason told Smith, "and tell Paul about what happened. I'll see if Della Street has anything on her mind and then come back."

Mason walked down to his office, latchkeyed the door, found Della Street standing in front of the mirror.

"Hello," she said. "I just got here."

"How come?" Mason asked.

"I rang the unlisted phone in your apartment, no answer. I rang Paul and he said you were out on a hot lead. I thought I'd come up and see if you needed anything."

"Good girl," Mason told her. "We're working on something hot."

"What is it?"

"Robert Selkirk. The way things look now, his mother and his stepfather left him alone while they went to the airport to meet Norda Allison. Robert was sleeping in a tent in the patio. It's beginning to look as though Robert got frightened, sneaked into the house, took possession of that .22 Colt Woodsman, then went back to bed in his tent in the patio. Sometime in the night he was aroused by someone prowling around. That just could have been Mervin Selkirk who was engaged in planting that printing press in the Jennings' storeroom.

"Evidently the dog they keep knew Mervin Selkirk well enough so he let Selkirk prowl around the place as a friend. Whoever it was, it was someone the dog knew.

"Robert got frightened and took a shot in the dark.

That shot probably hit the boy's father. He left a blood trail all the way to his automobile, drove to the country club and died before he could get out of the car.

"Barton Jennings was supposed to take Robert to this camping expedition where the boys were going with their dogs. So he was able to ditch the dog somewhere, probably at a boarding kennel, and take Robert up to another baby sitter the boy knew. He did all that before five o'clock in the morning."

"Good heavens," Della Street said, "you mean the boy killed his own father?"

"It was an accident," Mason said. "Now then, Barton Jennings is giving the boy a good brain-washing. He's making Robert think it was all a nightmare, some hideous dream that he had in which he dreamed that he had pulled the trigger on the gun.

"In order to keep the boy from being called as a witness, they're trying to spirit him out of the country. By the time anyone can get the boy back as a witness, the kid will be convinced he may have had a nightmare but that he didn't actually pull the trigger on the gun."

Della Street watched Mason for a moment with thoughtful eyes. "So what do you do?" she asked.

Mason said, "I block the attempt. I get hold of the boy before his brain has been washed, and . . ." Suddenly his voice trailed off into silence.

"Exactly," Della Street said. "What's it going to do to a seven-year-old boy if he believes that he has killed his father?"

Mason started pacing the floor. "Hang it, Della," he said, "my duty is to my client. I can't sit back and let a client take a murder rap simply to spare the feelings of a seven-year-old boy. . . . And yet I can't have that seven-year-old boy dragged up in front of the authorities."

"As far as that's concerned, how are we going to prove our contention once we get him picked up?" Della Street asked.

Mason paced the floor, saying nothing.

"Can't you," she asked, "use the knowledge you have so you can drop a monkey wrench in the prosecutor's machinery and get Norda Allison acquitted without dragging the boy into it?"

"I'm darned if I know," Mason admitted, and then added, grinning, "of course, you *would* look at it from a woman's viewpoint and want to protect the child regardless of anything else."

"It's the right viewpoint," Della Street said.

"Come on," Mason said, changing the subject, "let's go down to Paul Drake's office and see what *he's* discovered."

He held the door open and the two of them walked down the echoing corridor of the deserted building to enter the offices of the Drake Detective Agency. Mason waved a greeting to the girl who was busy at the switchboard, held the gate open for Della Street and they walked down to Drake's office.

Drake was just hanging up one of his telephones as Mason and Della Street entered the office. Smithy was sitting in a corner of the office, scribbling in a notebook.

Drake said, "Well, we've traced your taxicab, Perry, we were lucky. One of my operatives picked up the trip on the dispatcher's records and managed to interview the driver. He was particularly impressed with the little boy. It happens he has a kid of his own and the youngster made quite an impression.

"Here's what happened: On the trip out to the airport the woman was telling the boy about going to Mexico City, all about Mexico and something about the history of Mexico City. She told him he'd see the famous Calendar Stone in the museum and quite a few things of that sort. The boy seemed to have something on his mind and she kept up quite a steady stream of conversation.

"They were going to take an American Airlines plane to Dallas and then from Dallas to Mexico City. He took them to the American Airlines.

"Now here's a peculiar thing. They never got on that plane."

"What plane?"

"The one on which they had reservations. Reservations had been made over the telephone for Mrs. Hallum and son. The reservations were confirmed all the way to Mexico City. They were told they would have to pick up their tickets thirty minutes before plane time and they promised to be there. They never showed up.

"The airlines felt certain there had been some unexpected delay in transportation to the airport and actually didn't sell out the reservations until the last minute. Then about five minutes before time of departure they had a couple of stand-bys and they put the stand-bys aboard the plane and wired Dallas to cancel the two tickets on the Mexico City flight unless other information was received."

"Then what happened to the woman and the child?" Mason asked. "Was it just an elaborate plant to throw us off the trail?"

"It could have been," Drake said, "but somehow I'm not so certain."

"Wasn't it unusual for the woman to be talking so much about Mexico City in the taxicab?" Della Street asked. "Wouldn't that indicate it was a plant?"

"It *might*," Drake said, "but the taxi driver felt certain it was on the up and up. Those taxi drivers get to handle a lot of people and become pretty darn good judges of human nature."

Mason nodded.

"Well," Drake asked, "what do we do?"

"Cover all the other airline offices," Mason said, "and see if the pair switched to another airline, and—"

"That's being done," Drake said, "but it's quite a job. I thought you'd want to know about the taxi driver right away."

Mason nodded.

One of the telephones on Drake's desk rang sharply.

Drake picked up the receiver, said, "Paul Drake talking," then frowned in thoughtful concentration as the receiver made a series of squawking noises which were audible throughout the room.

"Okay," he said, "that's a lead. Stay with it. Have you got a description of that man?"

Again Drake listened and then said, "See what you can do."

He hung up the phone, turned to Mason and Della Street and said, "Well, part of the mystery is clearing up.

"One of my operatives scouting for leads around the place found that a porter remembered the woman and the boy. He took their baggage to the weighing-in scales at the American Airlines desk. The woman and the boy went up to the ticket counter, then two men came up and talked with the woman—one man did most of the talking. He had an air of authority. Then they took the two suitcases off the weighing scales, and the two men, the woman and the boy walked out toward the curb.

"The porter didn't know what happened after that. He was hanging around because he expected a tip for handling the baggage and no one offered to tip him. Naturally he remembered the transaction."

"The devil!" Mason exclaimed.

"Police?" Smith asked.

"Could be," Drake said. "They acted with that unmistakable air of authority. The porter said he didn't think they looked like police."

"They don't any more," Mason commented thoughtfully. "Good police detectives look like bankers or sales executives."

Drake said, "Incidentally, Perry, I heard from the operative I sent up to the camp, where Robert and his dog were supposed to be."

"They weren't there?" Mason asked.

"Robert wasn't there. He never did show up at the starting point. My man had a wild-goose chase: took a trip by automobile, then transferred to saddle horse, rode five miles over mountain trails, got bitten by a dog, turned around and rode the five miles back. He says the only two places he isn't sore are on top of his head and the soles of his feet. He said that was some gathering of kids and dogs, mongrels, purebreds and general canines of all sizes. They'd started out with the dogs on leash, but after a while they just turned 'em loose. The guy in charge said they'd only had a couple of dog fights and then everything had worked out beautifully. The dogs seemed to enter into the spirit of the thing.

"The man in charge said Robert and his dog had been booked for the trip but hadn't shown up. There were seven kids in all."

Mason was thoughtful for a while, then said, "Keep a watch on Jennings, Paul. See what you can find out."

"Something in particular?" Drake asked.

"If they started for Mexico City," Mason said, "he undoubtedly arranged for some sort of a code signal, either by way of telephone or telegram, to let him know that they were safely outside the jurisdiction of the court. When he doesn't hear from them, he'll begin to get alarmed.

"In the meantime, if the police have moved in, they'll be trying to find out just what it is Robert Selkirk did and just what it is he knows. I'm going to apply for a writ of habeas corpus for Norda Allison tomorrow morning.

"If the police have Robert, there's no use trying to do anything more about him, but I sure would like to know whether they have him, and if so, what story they got. Any chance of finding out?"

Drake shook his head. "Not if they don't want you to know, Perry. They'll have Robert and the woman buried somewhere. They *may* tell Barton Jennings what has happened so he won't be too nervous."

"Suppose they do? Then what?" Mason asked.

"That'll mean they're all working hand in glove," Drake said.

"And if they don't?"

Drake grinned. "That'll mean Robert has told his story to the police and the police don't like it. Then they won't be so certain Norda Allison is guilty."

"Keep your operatives on Barton Jennings," Mason said, "and if he begins to get a little restive and nervous, we'll know that it's time to rush a preliminary hearing for my client."

Again the phone rang, again Drake picked up the receiver, said, "Hello," listened in frowning concentration, asked a couple of questions, hung up the telephone and turned to Perry Mason. "This," he said, "is completely cockeyed."

"What is?"

"The printing press on which envelopes had been addressed to Norda Allison was found where it had been concealed out in some brush at the San Sebastian Country Club. It was on a lower level of the hill on which the clubhouse is situated. It's about twenty yards from a service road which winds up to the back of the clubhouse through some thick brush. In an airline it's about two hundred yards from the place where the body of Mervin Selkirk was found, but it's out of sight of that location.

"And," Drake went on before Mason could make any reply, "in the middle of the inked circular steel disc on top of the printing press was found a very nice imprint of the right middle finger of Norda Allison."

"Well," Mason said, "*that* opens up a lot of interesting possibilities."

"Keep talking," Drake said.

Mason was thoughtful for a moment, then said, "If Norda Allison's story is true, she must have made that fingerprint on the printing press sometime early yesterday morning."

"And Mervin Selkirk was killed sometime around two or three o'clock, according to the best estimate the police can get at the moment," Drake said.

"Then the printing press must have been taken out to

the Country Club *after* Selkirk's death," Mason said. "This may give us an opportunity to drag Barton Jennings right into the middle of it."

Paul Drake said dryly, "You're overlooking one thing, Perry."

"What's that?"

"You're assuming your client is telling the truth about *when* that fingerprint got placed on the printing press."

"I always assume my clients are telling the truth."

"Yes, I know," Drake retorted, "but figure it out, Perry. Suppose she found the printing press in his car, took it out, drove down the service road and hid it in the brush."

Mason thought the thing over. "I think it's quite apparent now that someone is trying to frame my client."

"Famous last words," Drake said ironically. "Incidentally, Mervin Selkirk kept a room at the San Sebastian Country Club. He's been a member for several years. Two weeks ago he arranged for a room there. They have a couple of dozen they rent out, mostly on week ends. Mervin Selkirk said he wanted his by the month."

Mason thought over Paul Drake's statement, then abruptly turned to Della Street. "Come on, Della. We're going to see Horace Livermore Selkirk and suggest that *he* file habeas corpus proceedings to force the authorities to surrender his grandson, Robert Selkirk."

"You're going to tell him what you know?" Della Street asked.

"Not only that, but I'm going to tell him what I *surmise*," Mason said, grinning.

12

HORACE LIVERMORE SELKIRK'S HOUSE WAS SPREAD OUT
on the top of a sunny knoll.

The lower part of the knoll was parched and browned
by the California dry-season sunlight, but the upper part
which contained the house, the grounds and a small golf
course, was dark with shade, green with grass, cool
with the scent of growing vegetation. The house was of
stainless steel, glass and aluminum.

The driveway wound up the slope until it came to the
meshed wire fence which stretched a ten-foot barrier,
topped with barbed wire. A caretaker's cottage was just
outside the electrically operated gate and Mason's car
came to a stop where the road narrowed in front of the
gate.

The caretaker, a man in his early fifties with a deputy
sheriff's star pinned to his shirt, a belt with holstered
gun and shells, came to the door and surveyed Mason
and Della Street appraisingly.

"Perry Mason," the lawyer said, "and this is my secretary. We want to see Mr. Selkirk."

"What about?" the man asked.

"Mr. Selkirk will know when you mention the name."

"We don't disturb him unless we know what it's
about."

Mason fixed the guard with cold eyes. "It's about a
matter in which he is very much interested," he said. "I
am Perry Mason and I wouldn't have driven out here unless the matter was of considerable importance."

"Why didn't you telephone for an appointment?"

"Because I didn't choose to," Mason said. "I'm going

to put some cards on the table and the manner in which Mr. Selkirk receives my information will depend on how many cards I put down."

The man hesitated, said, "Just a minute," stepped inside the house and picked up a telephone.

He spoke briefly, then a moment later hung up the telephone and pressed a button.

The huge steel gates moved silently back on their heavy roller bearings. The caretaker motioned Mason on and the lawyer sent his car through the gates up along the scenic driveway to the parking place in front of the house.

Horace Selkirk came strolling out from the rear portion of a huge patio to meet his guests. The patio contained a swimming pool, a barbecue grate, a picnic table and luxurious lounging furniture.

The patio had been ingeniously designed so that it could be opened to the sun or completely roofed over and glassed in, if desired. Wet splotches on the cement indicated the pool had been in recent use. Two inflated inner tubes floated on the water. A toy boat had drifted to one side of the pool. A floating rubber horse nodded solemnly in the pool, actuated by a faint breeze. Highball glasses were on the table, one partially filled. Ice cubes in the glasses had melted down to about half size.

"How do you do?" Selkirk said, somewhat coldly. "This is rather an unexpected visit."

Mason said, "So it is."

"Usually," Selkirk said, "those desiring to consult with me telephone and ask for an appointment."

"So I would assume," Mason said.

Selkirk's eyes were frosty. "It is a procedure I like to encourage."

"Doubtless," Mason said. "However, since you seem so well versed as to *my* movements, I thought perhaps it would be unnecessary."

"I am not telepathic," Selkirk said.

"You said that you relied on the services of private detectives."

"I do."

"If *I* were having *you* shadowed," Mason told him, "I would know when you were coming to call on me."

"You think I'm having you shadowed?" Selkirk asked.

"Someone is," Mason said. "It was rather neatly done. I appreciate the technique."

"What do you mean?"

"The manner in which the shadowing was done. A casual appearance from time to time of two different cars which would pass me, then turn a corner, appear once more behind me and then again pass me. And at times in the city I would notice that I was being shadowed by a car which must have been running on a course parallel to my own, some two blocks distant. That is, I believe, electronic shadowing which is made possible by means of a small device fastened somewhere to the underside of my car, which emanates a certain radionic signal that can be picked up and located by the shadowing car—I'll have to have my car looked over by a mechanic, I suppose."

Selkirk suddenly threw back his head and laughed. "It won't do you any good, Mason. By the time you found one device, my men would have something else pinned on."

"And," Mason said, "I assume my car has been bugged so my conversations can be duly recorded?"

"No, no, not that," Selkirk protested. "We'd get into difficulties with that and besides, I would want you and your very estimable secretary to be able to discuss business matters in private without feeling that I was eavesdropping. But do come in.

"It's a little warm today but not really warm enough here in the patio where it's really delightful, just shirtsleeve weather, and if Miss Street has no objection you might as well slip off your coat and be comfortable."

"Thanks," Mason said, removing his coat.

Selkirk led the way to a shaded corner where a breeze blowing up the hill was somehow funneled through steel latticework to cool a deeply shaded L-shaped nook. Light filtered in through heavy plate-glass windows which had been tinted a dark green.

"I took the liberty of having a couple of mint juleps prepared for you," Selkirk said. "I was drinking one and I thought you and Miss Street would care to join me."

He indicated a table on which there was a tray and two frosted glasses decorated with sprigs of mint.

"Perfect hospitality," Mason said, as Della Street seated herself and picked up one of the glasses. "Next time you might telephone your guard that we're coming so that the gates can be opened."

Selkirk shook his head. "I trust my detectives, but not quite that far. I like to have visitors inspected before they arrive."

Selkirk tilted his glass toward his visitors. "Regards," he said.

Mason sipped the drink.

Selkirk raised his eyebrows inquiringly.

"Excellent," Mason said.

"Thank you. Now what was the object of your visit?"

"Your grandson," Mason said.

Selkirk's body became instantly motionless; his face was a frozen mask. The man seemed to be holding his breath, yet without displaying even a flicker of changing expression. "What about Robert?"

"His mother," Mason said, "seems to have arranged for him to be taken to Mexico City by a baby sitter named Grace Hallum."

"Mexico City?"

"Yes."

"Why?"

"Apparently because sometime Friday night Robert fired a Colt .22 Woodsman in the general direction of a prowler—or someone who was moving around outside his tent, perhaps with the idea of taking Robert away while his mother and Barton Jennings were at the airport greeting Norda Allison."

"Do you know this or do you surmise it?" Selkirk asked.

"I know it."

"How do you know it?"

"That is something else," Mason said. "I thought you would be interested in the information."

"They're in Mexico City?"

"No. I said that Robert's mother had arranged for him to be taken to Mexico City. I don't think they made it."

"What *do* you think happened?" Selkirk asked, still holding his glass motionless halfway to his lips, his body tense, leaning slightly forward, his eyes cold, hard and watchful.

"Detectives?"

"I think so," Mason said. "A porter remembers two men with that indefinable air of authority which sometimes characterizes police officers. They removed the baggage from the scales at the checking-in counter of American Airlines. Robert and Miss Hallum accompanied these two men."

Selkirk digested the information for a moment, then settled back in his chair, raised the mint julep glass and took a long sip of the cooling contents.

"Why did you come to me?" he asked after a moment.

Mason said, "It is possible that your grandson is being subjected to suggestion and repetitious assertion of certain things which he is told must have happened while he was asleep. There is also, of course, the possibility that your son was planning to take Robert outside the jurisdiction of the California courts before new guardianship or custody proceedings could be instituted, and that Robert, hearing a prowler, pointed and discharged Barton Jennings' .22-caliber automatic.

"In any event, there is persuasive evidence that the shot fired from the tent where Robert was sleeping found a human target."

"What sort of persuasive evidence?" Selkirk asked.

"A blood trail which led from the vicinity of the tent to the curb where a car was parked. The blood trail was removed, at least in part, by a stream of water played on the grass and the sidewalk through a hose early yesterday morning."

"Barton Jennings?"

Mason nodded.

Selkirk toyed with his glass for several seconds, his eyes hard with concentration, his face a mask.

"Just what do you expect me to do, Mason?"

"There are two things which can be done. You can do one. I can do the other."

"What would you suggest that *I* do?"

"As the child's grandfather, you might insist that the police detention is violating the law. You might allege that Grace Hallum was contributing to the delinquency of a minor in trying to lead your grandson to believe that he had fired the shot which had resulted in his father's death. You might file a writ of habeas corpus stating that Grace Hallum, an entirely unauthorized person, has the child in custody. This would force Lorraine Jennings, the child's mother, either to yield the point or to come out in the open and state that *she* had ordered the child removed from the jurisdiction of the court."

Selkirk thought the matter over for a moment, then said, "Just sit here and cool yourselves with these drinks. If you want a refill, just press that button. I'm going to telephone my legal department. Excuse me for a moment, please."

Selkirk took another swallow of his mint julep, put down the partially empty glass and walked around the corner of the L-shaped alcove. Presently they heard the sound of a heavy glass partition sliding on roller bearings.

Della Street started to say something. Mason motioned her to silence, said conversationally, "Nice place Selkirk has here."

"It must cost him a fortune to keep it up."

"He has a fortune."

"Why should he be having your car shadowed?"

"I wouldn't know," Mason said. "We weren't shadowed earlier in the day. However, that's entirely up to Selkirk. If he wants to spend his money on detectives, finding out where I go, it will at least be a bonanza for the detectives and will keep some of Selkirk's money in circulation."

Mason closed his eye in a broad wink to Della Street, then stretched, yawned and said sleepily, "I've been losing too much sleep lately. I guess there's nothing I can do from now on except . . . I guess we can afford to slow down until Norda Allison's preliminary hearing comes up . . . ho . . . ho . . . hummmm! This place certainly is relaxing. It's making me sleepy."

Once again Mason closed his eye in a broad wink.

"That mint julep hits the spot," Della Street said. "It also has a relaxing effect."

Mason said sleepily, "It does for a fact—well, Della, drink it up because as soon as Selkirk returns we're going to get away from here. We'll check with Paul Drake to see if there's anything new, then call it a day and I'll see you at the office in the morning."

"Aren't you going to finish your drink?" Della asked.

"I'm driving," Mason said. "The drink was so tempting I had to taste it, but I'm limiting myself to a couple of swallows. I have an aversion to drinking and driving."

"One drink isn't going to affect your driving," Della Street said.

"It isn't that so much," Mason told her, "as the fact that I dislike to lose lawsuits. Suppose someone runs into me at an intersection. He may have gone through a red light, may have been going too fast and have defective brakes, but an officer comes up to investigate, smells liquor on *my* breath and I tell him that I've had one mint julep. You know how a jury would react to that. They'd say, 'Yeh, the guy *admits* to having one. That means he must have had a dozen.' "

"Under those circumstances," Della Street said, "you can have the sole responsibility. *I'm* going to finish this drink. It's the most wonderful mint julep I've had in a long time."

"Thank you," Selkirk's voice said, as he came unexpectedly around the corner of the alcove. "I've telephoned my legal department, Mason, and they'll get on the job immediately."

"That's fine," Mason told him, getting to his feet. "Your relaxing atmosphere has made me drowsy."

"Care for a swim and a little relaxation by the pool?" Selkirk asked. "I have plenty of suits and dressing rooms."

"No, thank you," Mason told him. "I'm a working man and have to be on my way."

"I hope you and Miss Street come back again," Selkirk said, and then with his voice suddenly taking on an authoritative note, said, "And it will be better if you telephone."

"Thank you for the invitation," Mason told him.

They shook hands. Selkirk escorted them past the pool, to the parking space.

Della Street jumped in the car, slid under the steering wheel and over to the far side of the seat. Mason got in behind the steering wheel.

"Just drive right on through the other end of the parking place and around the circle," Selkirk said. "The gate will be open for you as you go out."

Mason nodded, swept the car into motion.

It was a neighborhood of rolling hills and vistas of country estates. Glistening white houses and hillside subdivisions met their eyes as they swung down the long driveway to the highway.

Mason made the boulevard stop, then put his car into

motion, swung over to the stream of fast-moving traffic and stepped on the throttle.

"You're very anxious to get where you're going, all of a sudden," Della Street said.

"Yes," Mason told her, "I have decided there's no use working too hard. Let's get where we can relax. I know a cocktail bar about a mile down the road. We can pull in there and—"

"But I thought you wouldn't have a drink when you were driving."

"I won't be driving for a while," Mason said. "We'll get in there where it's cool and dark and comfortable and forget about the case. There's nothing more I can do now until the matter comes up for the preliminary examination . . . not unless Paul Drake's men uncover some new information."

Della Street started to say something, then checked herself.

Mason drove silently until he came to a small hotel, said, "There's a parking lot here. We'll leave the car and go relax for a while. It will do us good."

He swung into the parking lot and led Della Street into the hotel.

"What in the world *are* you doing, Chief?" she asked.

"I don't know whether the car is bugged or not," Mason said. "But we do know one thing. They have it rigged up so they can follow us by using electronics. Quick, Della, right through the cocktail bar and . . . there's a taxi stand right outside and . . . thank heavens there's a taxi there."

Mason signaled a cab driver, caught Della Street's elbow in his hand, hurried her across to the taxicab, jumped in beside her, slammed the door shut and said to the driver, "Straight on down the street. I want to catch a party who just left here."

The driver put the cab into motion.

Mason, looking through the rear window, said, "Turn

to the left at the first street and then turn to the left once more."

The cab driver obediently followed instructions.

Della Street said in a low voice, "What's the idea, Chief?"

Mason said, "Horace Livermore Selkirk has Grace Hallum and Robert up there in the house with him."

"You're certain?" Della Street asked.

"Pretty certain," Mason said. "There was a toy boat in the swimming pool when we went in. When we came out it was no longer there. Horace Selkirk could well have been one of them with the aura of authority who stopped the trip to Mexico City."

Mason said to the cab driver, "Turn to the left once more and then to the right. I'll tell you where to go."

"But, Chief," Della Street protested, "we can't go back up there in a taxicab and even expect . . . Why, he won't let us inside the gates."

"That's true," Mason told her. "But I think he's afraid now that I'm suspicious and my best guess is he's going to get rid of the boy—after all, he's in a very vulnerable position."

"He is if he gets caught," Della Street said. "But . . . I'm afraid I don't get it."

"Well," Mason told her, "our car is hotter than a firecracker. He's got it bugged up so his private detectives can follow it. We put it in the parking place there at that hotel and cocktail lounge, and you can bet that his detectives followed right behind us. We went into the cocktail lounge and they probably watched where we were going, then went to telephone a report to Horace Selkirk.

"We fooled them by going right on through and jumping in a cab. There's a good chance they didn't even see us take the cab. If they did, they didn't have a chance to follow us because there's no one on our tail now, and they certainly don't have these cabs bugged so they can be followed by electronics—it is, of course, taking a chance but it's a chance worth taking. If we hit anything, we hit the jackpot. If we lose out, we're out the price of one taxi trip and we can go back and sit in the cocktail lounge for an hour or so, and then lead Horace Livermore Selkirk's spies back to the office."

"They'll tell him we took a taxi ride?" Della Street asked.

Mason shook his head. "They won't be certain just *what* we did. Therefore, they'll simply state, 'Subjects parked their car, entered the hotel, went into the cocktail lounge and emerged two hours later to get in their car and drive to the office.'

"Later on, if it should appear that the point was important, they would say, 'Why, yes, we missed them for half an hour or so but we assumed they were around the hotel somewhere because their car was there so we didn't consider the matter worthwhile reporting.' On a shadow job of that kind, you can't stand right at the subject's elbow all the time.

"Turn off up here at the right," Mason said to the cab driver after some ten minutes.

"That road doesn't go anywhere," the cab driver said, "except up to some private property. There's a gate—"

"I know," Mason told him, "but I'm expecting a person to meet me . . . slow down . . . slow down, cabbie. Get over to the side of the road and take it easy."

Mason nudged Della Street as a cab came down the road headed toward them. The cab passed them and they got a glimpse of a woman and a boy in the back seat.

Mason said to the cab driver, "I think that's the couple we want but I can't be certain of it until I get a closer look. Turn around and follow that cab. Let's see if we can get a closer look and find out where they're going."

"Say, what is this?" the cab driver asked.

"It's all right," Mason told him, "you're driving a cab."

"That's *all* I'm doing. I'm not mixing in any rough stuff," the driver said.

"Neither am I," Mason assured him. "Just keep that cab

in sight. I want to find out where it goes. If you're really interested, I'm getting evidence in a divorce case. Here's twenty bucks. Any time you don't like the job, quit it, but when you get finished, if you make a *good* job of it, you get another twenty on top of this. Now are you satisfied?"

"I'm satisfied," the driver said, and accelerated the car.

"Not too fast," Mason warned. "I don't want them to get nervous."

"They're looking straight ahead," the driver said, "but the cabbie up front will spot me. A good cab driver keeps his eye on the rearview mirror from time to time."

"Fix it so he doesn't notice you," Mason said. "Don't drive at a regular distance behind him. Where there's not much chance he's going to turn off, drop way behind, then close the gap when you get into traffic."

The driver handled the car skillfully, keeping some distance behind the car in front until traffic thickened, then moving up and, from time to time, changing lanes so that the relative position of the two cars varied.

The cab ahead eventually came to a stop at a relatively small hotel. The woman and the child got out. The cab driver lifted out suitcases.

"Around the block and stop," Mason told the driver, handing him another twenty-dollar bill.

As soon as the cab rounded the corner, Mason had the door open. Della Street jumped out and the two hurried around the corner and into the hotel.

The well-tailored blond had just finished registering as Mason and Della Street approached the desk.

The clerk smacked his palm down on a call bell, said, "Front! . . . take Mrs. Halton to 619."

Mason approached the desk. "Do you have a J. C. Endicott in the house?" he asked the clerk.

The clerk frowned at him impatiently and motioned toward the room phone. "Ask the operator," he said.

Mason went to the room phone, picked up the receiver, said to the operator, "Do you have a Mr. J. C. Endicott in the house?"

"From where?" the operator asked.

"New York," Mason said.

There was a moment of silence; then she said, "I'm sorry. He doesn't seem to be registered."

"Thank you. That's all right," Mason said.

The lawyer hung up the telephone and walked across to where Della Street was waiting within earshot of the clerk.

"He's in," Mason told her. "He says for us to come right up. Boy, it's sure going to seem good to see good old Jim and hear all about that hunting trip."

He led Della Street to the elevators, said, "Seventh floor, please," and then after the cage came to a stop, led Della Street to the stair door. They opened the door, walked down one flight to the sixth floor.

The bellboy who had taken the woman and the boy up to 619 was just getting aboard the elevator on the way down when Mason and Della Street entered the sixth floor hallway. They walked down to 619 and Mason tapped on the door.

"Say it's the maid with soap and towels," Mason said to Della Street in a whisper.

After a moment of silence, a woman's voice on the other side of the door said, "Who is it, please?"

"Maid, with soap and towels," Della Street said in a bored voice.

The door was unlocked and opened.

Della Street walked in, followed by Perry Mason.

They found themselves in a two-bedroom suite with a central parlor and two bedrooms.

Mason kicked the door shut and turned the bolt.

The tall blonde moved back, her eyes wide with alarm. alarm.

"Sit down, Mrs. Hallum," Mason said. "You're not going to get hurt if you tell the truth. Why didn't you go to Mexico City the way you were supposed to?"

"I . . . I . . . Who are you? What do you want? And—"

"I want to know why you didn't go to Mexico City," Mason said.

She bit her lip. "I suppose you're representing Mrs. Jennings. I . . . well . . . I've been wondering if what I did was right, but . . ."

"Go ahead," Mason said.

"I don't know as I should tell it to you."

"Want to talk with the police?" Mason asked, moving toward the telephone.

"No. Heavens, no! That's the one thing we must avoid at *all* costs."

"All right," Mason told her. "Talk to me."

He turned to Della Street who had taken a shorthand notebook from her purse. "Sit over at that table," he said. "Take down what she says. All right, Mrs. Hallum, let's have it."

She walked through to the connecting room, said, "Robert, you stay in there for a little while. Just sit down and wait until I come for you."

"Yes, ma'am," Robert said politely.

Mrs. Hallum came back and closed the door.

"Just what is it you want to know?" she asked.

Mason said, "You were supposed to take Robert to Mexico City. You didn't do it. Why?"

"Because his grandfather told me I'd be arrested if I did."

"And what did you do?"

"I accompanied him to his house up on the hill, then a short time ago he told me that I had to leave, that I was to go to this hotel, that rooms had been arranged for me."

"And why were you to take Robert to Mexico City?" Mason asked.

"Because," she said, "Robert . . ."

"Go on," Mason said.

"Robert may have killed his father," she said.

"And they want to keep Robert from finding that out?"

125

"They want to protect Robert until there can be a more complete investigation. Robert knows he shot somebody. It's a horrible thought for a child to have in his mind. He hasn't been told that his father is dead."

"What do *you* think?" Mason asked.

"I don't know," she said. "Barton Jennings, that's the man who married Robert's mother, keeps telling Robert that he mustn't worry, that it was just a dream. He can't quite convince Robert that it was."

"How did Robert happen to have the gun?" Mason asked.

"His mother had a baby sitter who let him play with the gun. She would always unload it before she gave it to him. The boy had a habit of looking at Western pictures and Western shows. He feels a gun is a symbol of protection, of security, of manhood. He's nervous and sensitive and—well, he's resourceful."

"Go on," Mason said.

"It wasn't long before Robert wanted a loaded gun. Without this baby sitter, a Mrs. Hannah Bass, knowing any thing about it, he got hold of a .22-caliber cartridge. He'd amuse himself by putting that shell in the magazine, then working the recoil mechanism by hand.

"About a week ago Mr. Jennings, the boy's stepfather, found Robert had been playing with the gun. At first he was angry, but then he got over it.

"Friday night they both drove to the airport. Robert knew they were going and hadn't been able to get a baby sitter. They told him they'd only be gone for an hour.

"Robert asked for the gun and Mr. Jennings let him put it under his pillow in the tent in the patio. Robert loaded the gun with the .22 cartridge and put it under his pillow.

"I've never seen a boy with such an obsession about guns."

"All right," Mason said. "What happened Friday night?"

"Robert must have had a nightmare. He says he heard

steps coming toward his tent, then he saw the form of a big man looming in the doorway. He says he groped for the gun—and it went off. He really wasn't conscious of pulling the trigger, but there was the roar of an explosion, then he heard somebody running away. Robert says he fired the gun. I'm not certain but what someone else, standing just outside the tent, fired a shot. That's my own idea for what it's worth. Mr. Jennings says Robert should be led to believe it was all a bad dream. Robert knows better.

"Of course, Robert was only half-conscious at the time. He knows he was holding the gun. He thinks he fired it. Probably he could be made to think it was a dream. Mr. Jennings thinks it can be managed."

"What did Robert do after the shot?"

"He ran into the house and wakened his mother. She told him Barton Jennings was asleep and had been suffering pain from his arthritis. She told Robert his stepfather had taken medicine to deaden the pain, had gone to sleep and mustn't be wakened. She told Robert that it was simply an accident; that accidents happen to everyone; that if Robert had heard somebody running away it meant that he had only frightened someone and hadn't hurt the man. Robert was reassured. After a while he was persuaded to go back to the tent.

"Mrs. Jennings took the empty gun and started to take it back upstairs to put it where it belonged, then remembered a guest, Norda Allison, was in the room. So she left the gun on the stand in the front hall at the foot of the stairs and went back to bed."

"Where was her husband?" Mason asked.

"Asleep in another downstairs bedroom. When he has his attacks of arthritis, he takes codeine and sleeps in a separate room."

"How did he find out about it?" the lawyer asked.

"Mrs. Jennings was worried. She slept for an hour or two and then wakened and couldn't go back to sleep. She heard her husband moving around in his room. That was about daylight. She went to him and told him what had happened. He became very much alarmed. He went out to look around and evidently found something which caused him great concern. He told Mrs. Jennings to take the gun from the place where she had left it on the hall stand and as soon as Norda Allison got up to return it to the drawer where they kept it. Then Mr. Jennings took Robert and brought him to me. I kept Robert all day yesterday and reassured him as best I could. Mr. Jennings said I should do a job of brain washing.

"Then this morning Mr. Jennings brought some of Robert's clothes to me and said I was to leave at once and take Robert to Mexico City. He said we had reservations at the Hotel Reforma. He gave me money for the fare, told me that we had reservations on a plane and everything was all cared for. We were to leave this morning.

"So we went down to the airport and Mr. Horace Selkirk, the boy's grandfather, showed up. I had never met him, but he identified himself to me and told me that under no circumstances was Robert to leave the jurisdiction of the court. He said we were to come with him and that he would take the responsibility. He said he would send for Barton Jennings and get the thing straightened out.

"He had a man with him and they put us in an automobile and took us up to Horace Selkirk's big house. Robert was happy there but I was worried because Mr. Jennings didn't show up to tell me that I had done the right thing.

"I took Robert in swimming and he had a wonderful time in the pool. He's visited there several times and always has the time of his life. His grandfather keeps toys and things for him and Robert loves it.

"Well, almost as soon as we had finished dressing after our swim Mr. Selkirk came rushing in to the rooms he had assigned us in the west wing of the house. He was very excited and said we were to pack up at once, get ready to leave and were to come here and wait here until he gave us further orders."

"What about Barton Jennings?" Mason asked. "Did he ever find out you weren't going to Mexico City?"

"No. Mr. Horace Selkirk had us write postal cards which he said would be flown to Mexico City and then mailed to Mr. and Mrs. Jennings. He told us that police were questioning the Jennings and that it was absolutely essential that we remain concealed so no one would know where we were. We had an understanding with Mr. Jennings that we would send postal cards that would simply be signed G.R. That stood for Grace and Robert."

"And you wrote some of those cards?"

"Yes."

"How many?"

"There must have been a dozen or so. Horace Selkirk almost threw them at us. He said he'd have them sent to Mexico City and mailed at intervals so no one would become suspicious. He had me scrawling postal cards until I became dizzy."

Mason studied her carefully for a moment, then said, "All right, now tell me the rest of it."

"What do you mean?"

"There's something else. How much did Selkirk promise you, or how much did he give you?"

She lowered her eyes.

Mason stood silent, his eyes steady, waiting.

At length she sighed, raised her eyes. "He gave me a thousand in cash and promised me five thousand more if I followed instructions."

Mason thought things over for a moment, then said, "Ever hear about the kidnaping law?"

"What do you mean?" she flared. "He's the boy's grandfather!"

"And as such has no more to say about his custody than anyone you'd meet on the street," Mason said. "Right at the moment the child's mother is the only one who has any say about where he's to be kept. She told you to take him to Mexico City."

"It was her husband who told me."

"But he was speaking for her. You were given custody of the boy to take him to Mexico City. If you take him anywhere else it's kidnaping."

"Mr. Selkirk said he'd fix it up with the Jennings."

"And did he do so?"

"He said he would."

"Then why promise you money?"

She was silent for several seconds. Then abruptly she said, "I knew I was doing something wrong. Okay, you win. I'm going to Mexico City."

"That's better," Mason told her. I'm going down and get a taxicab. Give me your suitcases. This is Miss Street, my secretary. We'll take the suitcases down and handle things so no one will know you checked out. You wait exactly twenty minutes, then take Robert, go down in the elevator, ask if there's a drugstore near here, walk out of the hotel and turn to the right. Miss Street and I will be waiting in a taxicab on the corner. You've made a wise decision. We must keep Robert away from all these emotional stresses. Now you go to Mexico where you can take Robert's mind off what has happened. It's particularly important you stay where Horace Selkirk won't know where you are."

"But how can we do that?" Grace Hallum asked. "He'll be furious. He'll find us."

Mason said, "No, he won't. You'll be at the one place where he'd never expect you to be. The Hotel Reforma in Mexico City."

Grace Hallum said, "The suitcases are all packed. We haven't unpacked. We just got here."

Mason nodded to Della Street, said, "If you don't mind, we'll take the suitcases to another floor. We don't want it to appear that *you're* checking out."

"But what about the bill on these two rooms?"

"The reservations were made by Horace Livermore Selkirk," Mason said. "Let him pay the bill."

"How long will it be before anyone finds out we're not here?"

Mason grinned. "It *could* be a long time."

"And then?" she asked.

"Then," Mason said, "when Horace Livermore Selkirk finally puts two and two together, he may quit being so damned patronizing."

13

BACK IN THE COCKTAIL LOUNGE AT THE HOTEL WHERE they had engaged the cab Mason said to Della, "I think those are our shadows over there."

"Where?"

"The man and the woman in the corner. There have been surreptitious glances in our direction, and the man's not as interested in her as he should be in an attractive woman companion who is being plied with liquor."

"Why plied?" Della Street asked.

"It makes them pliable," Mason said.

She laughed. "Ever try it?"

"What we need," Mason told her, "is a red herring. Go to the phone booth, call Paul Drake and tell him we want a woman operative who is about twenty-seven blonde, rather tall, with a good figure, and a seven-year-old boy, well-dressed, quiet and dark."

"Why do we want them?" she asked.

"Because," Mason said, "we're going to give Horace Selkirk's detectives something to think about."

"And what do they do?" Della Street asked.

Mason said, "They move into the hotel where Horace

Selkirk got the two connecting rooms for Grace Hallum and Robert Selkirk. Drake can fix them up with a passkey and they can move right into the hotel as though they owned the place. Tell Paul not to ever let them charge anything, but to pay cash for everything. The woman isn't *ever* to sign the name of Grace Hallum. She's simply to pay cash for everything."

"But won't the clerk know the difference? That is, won't he—?"

"We'll wait until the night clerk comes on duty," Mason said, "then this operative and the boy will go into the hotel, take the key to 619 and 621, move in there and stay there.

"The woman is to keep the key to the room in her purse, never to go near the desk, never to say to anyone that she is Grace Hallum."

Della Street thought the matter over, then said, "You don't suppose they've got the line tapped here, do you?"

"I doubt it," Mason said. "It's a chance we'll have to take. Just go to the phone and call Paul. I'll keep an eye on the couple over there and see what they do."

Ten minutes later when Della Street was back, Mason said, "They were certainly interested in your telephone call, Della, but they didn't dare appear too curious. They're wondering what kept us out of circulation for so long—how did Paul Drake react?"

"The same way you'd expect," she said. "He agreed to do it, but he's not happy about it."

"Why isn't he happy?"

"Says he's violating the law."

"What law?"

"What law!" Della Street asked. "Good heavens, here's a woman who moves into some other woman's room in a hotel, and—"

"What do you mean?" Mason asked. "She isn't moving into any other woman's room. Grace Hallum has left the hotel."

"But she didn't pay her bill."

132

"The bill was already paid," Mason said. "Horace Selkirk arranged for that, and even if she *had* left the hotel without paying the bill, she would have been the one who defrauded the hotelkeeper. Drake's operative isn't defrauding anybody."

"But she's moving into a room in a hotel."

"Exactly," Mason said. "She's prepared to pay for the accommodations. The hotel keeps its rooms for rental to the public."

"But she didn't register."

"Is there any law that says she has to?"

"I think there is."

"Grace Hallum didn't register. She simply went and picked up the key. That means somebody had registered into those rooms and left instructions with the clerk that the key was to be delivered when a woman with a child asked for it."

"Well," she said, "Paul Drake wasn't happy."

"I didn't expect him to be happy," Mason said. "When you hire a detective you pay his price for services rendered. If he follows instructions, you can guarantee to keep him out of jail, but you can't guarantee to make him happy."

14

JUDGE HOMER F. KENT LOOKED DOWN AT THE PEOPLE assembled in the courtroom and said, "This is the time fixed for the preliminary hearing in the case of the People versus Norda Allison."

"Ready for the People," Manley Marshall, a trial deputy from the district attorney's office, said.

"Ready for the defendant," Perry Mason responded.

"Very well. Proceed," Judge Kent said.

Marshall, following a generally recognized pattern with the crisp efficiency of a man who knows both his case and his law, and is determined to see that no loophole is left open, called the caretaker at the San Sebastian Country Club.

The caretaker testified to noticing a car parked early on the morning of the eighteenth. He had thought nothing of it as occasionally golfers came early for a round of golf. Later on, at about eleven-thirty, one of the golfers had told him that there was someone out in one of the parked cars who apparently had been drinking and was sound asleep.

The caretaker looked, saw the figure slumped over the wheel, did nothing about it for another hour. Then he had taken another look, had seen blood on the floor of the car and had notified the police.

"Cross-examine," Marshall said to Mason.

"Did you," Mason asked, "look inside the car?"

"I looked inside the car," the witness said.

"Did you open the door?"

"I did not open the door. I looked in through the glass window in the door."

"Through the glass window in the door?"

"Yes."

"Then the glass window in the door was rolled up?"

"I think so."

"That's all," Mason said.

Marshall called the deputy coroner who testified to being called to the scene, a photographer who introduced photographs, an autopsy surgeon who testified that death had been caused by a .22-caliber bullet. The bullet had entered on the left side of the chest, just in front of the left arm. It had ranged slightly backward and had lodged in the chest and had not gone all the way through the body. The autopsy surgeon had recovered the bullet and had turned it over to Alexander Redfield, the ballistics expert. Death, in the opinion of the physician, had not been instantaneous. There had been a period of consciousness and a period of hemorrhage. That period was, in his opinion, somewhat indefinite. It might have been an interval of ten or fifteen minutes after the shot had been fired and before death took place; it might have been only a minute or two.

"Cross-examine," Marshall said to Perry Mason.

"With reference to this indeterminate interval," Mason said, "it is then possible that the decedent had sustained the fatal wound at some other place and had driven the car to the place where the body was found?"

"It is possible but not probable."

"Would you say that the interval between the time the fatal wound was sustained and death could not have been more than ten minutes?"

"It could have been as much as ten minutes."

"Could it have been more?"

"I don't think so."

"Could it have been eleven minutes?"

"Well, yes. When I say ten minutes I am not referring to an interval which I time with a stop watch."

"Well, you know how long ten minutes is, don't you?" Mason asked.

"Yes."

"Now you say it could have been eleven minutes."

"It could have been."

"Twelve?"

"Possibly."

"Thirteen?"

"Well, yes."

"Fourteen?"

"I can't fix the time exactly, Mr. Mason."

"Fifteen?"

"I'm not going to say that it couldn't have been fifteen minutes."

"Twenty?"

"I doubt very much if it was twenty minutes."

"It could have been?"

"It could have been."

"The decedent could have been driving the car during that time?"

"During at least a part of that time. There was considerable hemorrhage and he was losing blood and losing strength."

"Thank you," Mason said. "That's all."

The doctor left the stand, and Marshall called Sergeant Holcomb to the stand.

Sergeant Holcomb testified that he was connected with the homicide squad of the police department; that he had gone to the San Sebastian Country Club, had examined the body and the car.

"Did you make any examination of the surrounding terrain?" Marshall asked.

"I did."

"Did you find anything which you considered significant?"

"I did."

"Please tell us what it was that you found."

Sergeant Holcomb glanced triumphantly at Perry Mason. "Concealed in the brush, within a hundred yards of the place where the automobile was parked, and just a few yards off a service road which skirts the hill on a lower level, I found a printing press."

"What sort of a printing press?" Marshall asked.

"A portable printing press of a very good quality which was capable of doing good work. It weighed in the vicinity of eighty-five pounds, I would say."

"What else can you tell us about that printing press, Sergeant?"

"A name and address had been set in type in that press. The name was the name of the defendant in this case and the address was her address in San Francisco."

"Did you find anything else significant about that printing press?"

"I did."

"What?"

136

"There was the imprint of a fingerprint in the ink on the steel table over which the rollers ran when the press was operated."

"That was a circular table?"

"It was."

"And it revolved with each impulse of the press; that is, each time the press was used the round steel table revolved?"

"It did."

"And there was black ink on this round steel plate?"

"There was."

"Can you describe that ink?"

"It is a very thick, sticky ink such as is used in printing presses of that type. When the rollers move over the steel table the ink clings to the rollers; that is, a small coating of ink clings to the rollers, and then as the rollers go down over the type, the type is inked just enough to make a legible print on the paper."

"That ink was thick enough and sticky enough to hold a fingerprint?"

"It held it very well, yes, sir."

"And were you able to identify the fingerprint which was on that table?"

"Yes, sir, absolutely."

"Whose print was it?"

"It was the print of the middle finger of the defendant in this case."

"Now then, Sergeant Holcomb, you described the operation of the press. Do I understand that whenever this press was put in operation the rollers moved over this steel table?"

"Yes, sir."

"And the table itself revolved?"

"Well, it didn't make a complete revolution, but it moved a few degrees of arc."

"Then, as I understand it, if the press had been actuated after that print had been made, the print would have been obliterated by the joint action of the rubber rollers, of which I believe there are two, and the rotation of the steel table?"

"That is correct."

"Did you find anything else in your search of the premises, Sergeant Holcomb?"

"I did."

"What?"

"I found an empty cartridge case."

"What sort of a cartridge case?"

"A .22-caliber cartridge case."

"Do you have that with you?"

"I do."

Sergeant Holcomb produced an envelope from his pocket, opened it, took out a small glass bottle which contained an empty .22-caliber cartridge case.

"This you found where?"

"At a point about twenty feet, as nearly as we could tell, twenty feet and two inches from the steering wheel of the automobile in which the body of Mervin Selkirk was found."

"What was the nature of the terrain at that point?"

"At that particular point the terrain was grassy. There was a practice putting green bordering the side of the parking space on the north. This cartridge case was in the grass. On the south side of the parking space there was native brush on the slope of the hill."

"That's all," Marshall said. "You may inquire, Mr. Mason."

Mason's smile was affable. "How long had this cartridge case been there in the grass before you picked it up, Sergeant?"

"If it had held the murder bullet, it couldn't have been there more than about twelve hours."

"*If* it had held the murder bullet?"

"Yes."

"Had it held that bullet?"

"I think it had."

"Do you *know* it had?"

"Well we can prove it by inference."

"Do you *know* it had?"

"No."

"Do you *know* how long the cartridge case had been there before you picked it up?"

"No, of course not. I wasn't there when the cartridge was fired. If I had been—"

"Could it have been there *two* days, Sergeant?"

"I suppose so."

"Ten days?"

"I suppose so."

"What was the nature of the terrain where you found the printing press?" Mason asked.

"It was on the sloping hill. The terrain there was covered with native brush."

"Where was the printing press, with relation to the brush; in deep brush or relatively in the open?"

"In deep brush."

"Was it sitting straight up or was it on an angle, as would have been the case if it had been thrown into the brush?"

"It was sitting straight up."

"As though it had been carefully placed there?"

"I can't say as to that. It was sitting straight up."

"And the fingerprint of the defendant was not smudged in any way?"

"No, sir, it was a perfect print."

"Did you find any other prints on the press?"

"Well, I didn't process the press myself. The fingerprint expert did."

"In your presence?"

"Yes, in my presence and in the presence of Lieutenant Tragg."

"Also of Homicide?"

"Yes."

"Were any other prints of the defendant found?"

"None that I know of."

"Would it have been possible for a woman of the build

of the defendant to have picked up an eighty-five pound printing press of this sort and transported it into the brush without leaving fingerprints on it?"

"Certainly. She could have used gloves."

"Yes, there were places where the brush had been trampled, that some person had gone in there carrying a heavy object?"

"Yes, there were places where the brush had been broken."

"Could you get any footprints?"

"No."

"Now, Sergeant, you're an expert crime investigator."

"I consider myself such."

"In transporting an object awkward to carry, such as a printing press of that sort, the transportation of that heavy, unwieldy object would have been attended with some difficulty?"

"I would say so."

"And do you consider that the press was placed there at night?"

"I don't know."

"It is a possibility?"

"Yes."

"It is a probability?"

"Yes."

"Moving in the dark that way, through a brushy terrain, there was quite a possibility the person would have stumbled?"

"Perhaps, if the press had been transported in the dark, but we don't know that it happened in the dark."

"It is a reasonable surmise?"

"I wouldn't say so."

"Pardon me, I must have misunderstood you."

"I said that it was a reasonable surmise that the press had been transported at night, but that didn't mean in the dark."

"Why not?"

"The person could have used a flashlight."

"I see," Mason said. "Holding an eighty-five pound printing press in one hand and a flashlight in the other?"

"Well, I didn't say that."

"Where would such a person have held the flashlight—in his teeth?"

"She could have held it in her mouth," Sergeant Holcomb said.

"I see," Mason said. "You are assuming that the defendant transported the press to this place of concealment."

"Yes."

"She did that, in your opinion, in order to conceal the press?"

"Naturally."

"She carried this eighty-five pound press in her hands and a flashlight in her teeth?"

"So I would assume."

"There would have been ink on the rollers?"

"Yes."

"And ink on the edges of the steel table?"

"To some extent, yes."

"And isn't it a fact that in picking up the press, the edges of the steel table would have pressed against the forearms of the person picking it up?"

"They might."

"And that would have left ink on the garments of the defendant, if *she* had been carrying it?"

"She might have been wearing short sleeves."

"At night?"

"Yes."

"And it would have been difficult to have transported that press through the brush at night without stumbling and falling?"

"I don't know."

"You didn't make a test to determine that?"

"Well, not exactly."

"You were the one who found the press?"

"I was," Sergeant Holcomb said, beaming with pride.

"And when you found it, were there other persons present?"

"Yes, sir."

"Who?"

"Two technicians and Lieutenant Tragg."

"And did you call to them to come and see what you had found?"

"Yes."

"And they came over to where you were standing in the brush?"

"Yes."

"And did any of them stumble?"

"Lieutenant Tragg caught his foot and fell flat."

"Did any of the others stumble?"

"The fingerprint man almost fell."

"Neither of these people were carrying anything?"

"No."

"And it was daylight?"

"Now, if the defendant had been trying to conceal the printing press, Sergeant, why would she have concealed it so near the scene of the crime?"

"You'd better ask her," Sergeant Holcomb said. "She's your client."

"That will do," Judge Kent said sharply. "There will be no repartee between witness and counsel. Answer the question."

"I think, if the Court please," Marshall said, "the question is argumentative and not proper cross-examination."

"It certainly is argumentative," Judge Kent said. "I was wondering if there would be an objection on that ground. The objection is sustained."

"Assuming," Mason said, "that some person, either the defendant or someone else, murdered Mervin Selkirk at the place where his car was parked, it is obvious that the murderer must have made an escape, presumably by automobile. Did you check the vicinity for the tire tracks of another automobile, Sergeant?"

"Certainly," Sergeant Holcomb said sneeringly. "We don't overlook the obvious."

"And did you find any such tracks?"

"We did not. The parking place was hard-topped and there were no other significant tire tracks that we could find."

"Did I understand you to say you didn't overlook the obvious?" Mason asked.

"That is quite correct," Sergeant Holcomb said.

"Then how did it happen that you overlooked the obvious fact that if a person had wanted to conceal the printing press, the murderer would have taken it away in the escape car rather than leave it in the brush within a hundred yards of the decedent's body where it was certain to be discovered?"

"That question is objected to as argumentative," Marshall said.

Judge Kent smiled faintly.

"The question was asked because of the statement of the witness that the police didn't overlook the obvious," Mason observed.

This time Judge Kent's smile broadened. "That was a statement which the witness shouldn't have volunteered," he said. "And, while it is a temptation to overrule the objection because of the manner in which the assertion was volunteered, the Court will sustain the objection to this present question on the ground that it is argumentative."

Judge Kent looked at Perry Mason, inclined his head slightly and said, "However, the parties will note that counsel has made his point."

"Thank you, Your Honor," Mason said. "That is all."

Marshall called Lieutenant Tragg to the stand.

"Lieutenant Tragg, did you make any search of the room which had been occupied by the defendant on the seventeenth and eighteenth; that is, Friday night and Saturday morning?"

"I did, yes, sir."

"What did you find, if anything?"

"Under the pillow of the bed I found a .22-caliber Colt automatic of the type known as a Colt Woodsman, number 21323-S."

"Do you have that weapon with you?" Marshall asked.

"I do."

"Will you produce it, please?"

Lieutenant Tragg opened a briefcase which he had taken in with him, and produced the weapon.

"Were there any fingerprints on this weapon?" Marshall asked.

"None that we were able to use; that is, none that were legible."

"Does the fact that there were no fingerprints on the weapon indicate to you that the fingerprints had been removed?"

"No, sir."

"Why not?"

"Because it is rather unusual to find fingerprints on a weapon of this type. The surface is usually somewhat oily and it is the exception rather than the rule to find any fingerprints. There is, however, one place where fingerprints are *sometimes* found. That is on the magazine clip. The clip is usually grasped between the thumb and forefinger and then pushed into place with the ball of the thumb. The magazine clip is not as oily as a rule as the rest of the gun, and sometimes we do find prints on the magazine."

"Did you find any prints on the magazine of this weapon?"

"None that we could use."

"Now, can you tell us exactly where you found this weapon?"

"Yes, sir. I found it under the pillow of the bed in the front room of the house occupied by Barton and Lorraine Jennings."

"Do you know that this was a room occupied by the defendant?"

"Not of my own knowledge, no, sir. I know only that it was a room in the front of the house, and I know that the defendant had at one time been in that room."

"How do you know that?"

"Her fingerprints were in various parts of the room, on doorknobs, by a mirror, on a table top and in other places."

"Did you photograph the exact position of the gun after the pillows had been removed?"

"I did."

"Do you have that photograph with you, or a copy of it?"

"I do."

"May I see it, please."

Tragg produced a photograph from the briefcase. Marshall stepped to the witness stand to take it from the witness, showed it to Perry Mason and said, "I would like to introduce this photograph in evidence."

The photograph showed the head of a bed, a rumpled sheet, two pillows and an automatic lying on the rumpled sheet.

"No objections," Mason said. "It may be received in evidence."

"Cross-examine the witness," Marshall said.

"I take it, Lieutenant Tragg," Mason said, "that the pillows which are shown in the photograph had been moved prior to the time the photograph was taken?"

"Yes, sir."

"But the gun was in exactly the same position that it was when you found it?"

"Yes, sir."

"Then, in removing the pillows, the gun was not disturbed?"

"No, sir."

"In removing those pillows then, you were looking for a weapon, were you not?"

"We hoped to find a weapon, yes."

"Was that gun loaded or unloaded when it was found?" Mason asked.

"It was unloaded. It had been unloaded."

"How do you know it had been unloaded?"

"Because of things that had been done to the barrel."

"There was no shell in the firing chamber?"

"No."

"None in the magazine?"

"No."

"Were there shells in the bedroom where the defendant had left her fingerprints?"

"Yes. There was a partially filled box of .22 shells."

"Did you find any fingerprints on that box of shells?"

"None that we could positively identify."

"That's all," Mason said.

"If the Court please," Marshall said, "Lieutenant Tragg can, of course, corroborate the finding of the empty cartridge case and the finding of the printing press, but I didn't ask him about those matters because this is merely a preliminary hearing and since Sergeant Holcomb has already given his testimony I see no reason in cluttering up the record. I will state, however, to counsel that if he desires to cross-examine Lieutenant Tragg upon these matters we have no objection."

"I have only one question on cross-examination in regard to that phase of the case," Mason said.

He turned to Lieutenant Tragg. "Do you think it would be possible to pick up the printing press in question without getting some smears of ink on your clothing?"

"It would be possible," Lieutenant Tragg said.

"But it would require some care in order to avoid doing so?"

"It would."

"Who carried the printing press out from its place of concealment to the car which eventually transported it to police headquarters?"

"I did."

"Did you get ink on your clothing?"

"Unfortunately, I did."

"You have heard Sergeant Holcomb's testimony about your falling through the brush?"

"Yes, sir."

"Did you fall?"

"I fell."

"Did you fall going out with the printing press?"

"No, sir, I used great care."

"But it was daylight?"

"It was daylight."

"In your opinion, Lieutenant Tragg, as an officer, was the printing press placed in a position of concealment where it was reasonably safe from detection?"

Marshall started to get to his feet and object, then changed his mind and sat back in his chair, quite evidently feeling Tragg could take care of himself.

"It wouldn't be safe from detection in the sort of examination which is usually made in a homicide case."

"In other words, you don't join with Sergeant Holcomb in considering that his discovery of the printing press represented an epochal achievement in the chronicles of crime detection?"

There was a ripple of laughter in the courtroom and this time Marshall, on his feet, angrily objected.

"The objection is sustained," Judge Kent said, but again there was a ghost of a twinkle in his eyes.

"No further questions," Mason said.

"We ask that the .22 Colt automatic, number 21323-S be received in evidence," Marshall said.

"No objection," Mason said.

"Call Alexander Redfield," Marshall said.

Redfield, the ballistics and firearms expert, came forward, was sworn and qualified himself as an expert.

Having been the victim of some of Mason's ingenious cross-examination several times in the past, the expert was exceedingly careful in answering questions.

"I show you a Colt Woodsman automatic, number 21323-S, which has been received in evidence," Marshall said, "and ask you if you have conducted a series of experiments with that weapon and if you have examined it."

"I have."

"I show you a .22-caliber bullet which has been received in evidence and which the testimony shows was the so-called fatal bullet taken from the body of Mervin Selkirk, and ask you if you have examined that bullet."

"I have."

"Did that bullet come from this gun?" Marshall asked.

"I don't know."

"You don't know?"

"No, sir. I know that it was fired from a weapon made by the Colt Manufacturing Company similar to this weapon, but I can't say that it came from this particular weapon."

"Why not? Can't you usually tell whether a given bullet comes from a given weapon?"

"Usually you can tell."

"How?"

"There are certain characteristics which are known as class characteristics," Redfield said. "Those relate to the pitch of the lands in the barrel, the dimension of the lands and grooves, the direction in which they turn, the angle of turn which gives a twist or rotation to the bullet, and from those class characteristics we can generally tell the make of weapon from which the bullet was fired.

"In addition to these general or class characteristics there are characteristics which are known as individual characteristics. Those are little striations which are found on a bullet, and are caused by individualized markings in the barrel itself. By comparing these markings, we are able to tell whether the striations on a fatal bullet coincide with those on a test bullet fired through a weapon, and from that we are able to determine whether a bullet was fired from a certain weapon."

"But you are unable to make that determination in the present case?"

"Yes."

"Why?"

"Because the barrel of the gun number 21323-S has been tampered with."

"What do you mean by being tampered with?"

"That's the best way I can explain it. It is as though someone had taken a small circular file of the type known as a rattail file, and scratched and filed the interior of the barrel so that the characteristics were entirely altered; that is, the individual characteristics."

"In your opinion, that was done?"

"In my opinion, the barrel was tampered with, yes, sir."

"Do you know when?"

"After the last bullet had been fired through that barrel."

"How do you know that?"

"Because of bits of metallic dust, or scrapings, which remained inside the barrel of the gun and the peculiar appearance of certain blemishes in the barrel which would have been altered in appearance by the firing of a bullet."

"Now then, I call your attention to the empty cartridge case introduced in evidence and found near the place where Mervin Selkirk's body was found. I ask you if you are able to tell whether that empty cartridge case had been fired in the gun in question."

"Yes. That cartridge was exploded or fired in the weapon which has been introduced in evidence."

"And how are you able to determine that?"

"By a microscopic examination of the imprint of the firing pin in the rim of the shell, and a microscopic examination of the ejector marks on the cartridge case."

"You may cross-examine," Marshall said to Mason.

"Did you check the ownership or registration of this weapon, number 21323-S?" Mason asked Redfield.

"I did. Yes, sir."

"And who is the registered owner of that weapon?"

"Mr. Barton Jennings."

"You found the weapon in his house?"

"Yes."

"And you found that the weapon was owned by him?"

"Yes, sir."

"Now, let me see if I understand your testimony," Mason said. "If the defendant in this case had killed Mervin Selkirk, she would have gone to a house owned by Barton Jennings, she would have found some way of possessing herself of a weapon belonging to Barton Jennings, she would then have left the house and gone to the San Sebastian Country Club; she would have fired a single shell which resulted in a fatal wound, bringing death to Mervin Selkirk, and then, regardless of whether she carried an eighty-five pound printing press out into the brush into the dark without stumbling, tearing her clothes, or getting ink all over her garments, she would have returned to her room in the Jennings house, would have taken a rattail file and spent some time working on the barrel of the gun so that the bullet could not be identified, and then would have conveniently left that gun under the pillow of the bed in which she had been sleeping so that you could find it there without any difficulty. Now my question is this, is there anything in your testimony that is inconsistent with such facts?"

"Your Honor, I object," Marshall said. "The question is argumentative. It assumes facts not in evidence. It is not proper cross-examination."

"The objection is overruled," Judge Kent said after some deliberation. "The question is skillfully framed. Counsel is asking the witness if certain things must have happened, whether his testimony indicates any evidence in contradiction of these facts. He is asking that question for the purpose of trying to clarify or modify the opinion testimony of an expert witness. I will permit the question only because this witness is an expert and for that one limited purpose."

Redfield said reluctantly, "I have no way of knowing

the sequence of the events or who altered the barrel of the gun. It is quite possible that the defendant could have left the gun under the pillow and that thereafter some other person could have altered the barrel by mutilating it with a rattail file."

"Exactly," Mason said, smiling. "Now we're coming to the point which I wish to bring out, Mr. Redfield. You state that you have no way of knowing who altered the barrel."

"That is correct."

"You assume that someone else could have done it."

"Yes, sir."

"That alteration of the barrel required the use of a long, thin, circular file of the type known as a rattail file?"

"Yes, sir."

"Do you know if any such implement was found in the possession of the defendant?"

"No, sir."

"It is not the type of implement that a woman would customarily carry in her purse?"

"Objected to as argumentative and calling for a conclusion of the witness," Marshall said. "The witness is an expert on firearms, not on women's purses."

"Sustained," Judge Kent ruled.

"But you have stated that it is quite possible that some other person, such as Barton Jennings for instance, took this weapon from under the pillow and mutilated the barrel with a rattail file and then replaced it?"

"Yes, sir."

"Now, isn't it equally plausible to assume," Mason said, "that the barrel of the weapon was mutilated and then it was placed under the pillow of the bed in which the defendant had slept, and that that was the first time the weapon had ever been in that bed."

"That, of course, is an assumption which *can* be drawn," Redfield said.

"A weapon of this sort placed upon a sheet leaves a certain imprint?"

"It may."

"I call your attention to the photograph which has been introduced in evidence showing the weapon in place where it was found, and ask you if you can find any place on that sheet as shown in the photograph where it appears that the weapon could have previously reposed."

"It would have been virtually impossible to have picked the weapon up, mutilated the barrel and then restored it to the exact position from which it had been taken?"

"It would not have been impossible . . . well, that depends on what you mean by the *exact* position."

"I mean the exact position."

"Well, if you are talking about a thousandth of an inch, it would have been virtually impossible. But it *could* have been carefully placed so that it was in *virtually* the same position from which it had been taken."

Mason stepped forward and said, "I now hand you an empty cartridge case and ask you to compare that with the cartridge case which has previously been introduced in evidence and to examine carefully the mark of the firing pin and the marks made by the automatic ejector and ask you if it appears to you that both cartridges were fired from the weapon in question."

Redfield took the empty cartridge case which Mason handed him, took a magnifying glass from his pocket, studied it carefully, said, "I can't tell you, Mr. Mason, with such examination as I can make at this time. I can state that it has the external appearances of having been fired from this weapon, but in order to make certain I would have to make a very careful check of the impression left by the firing pin in the rim of the cartridge case."

"How long would that take?"

"Perhaps a couple of hours."

"I suggest that you do it," Mason said. "I also suggest that you take care to mark this cartridge case so that it can be identified again without confusion."

"Now just a moment," Marshall said. "I don't know what counsel is getting at, but this is the same old run-around. As far as this case is concerned, it doesn't make any difference where this empty cartridge case came from. It doesn't have any bearing on the case. It is incompetent, irrelevant and immaterial.

"It is, however, a well-known fact that in cases of this sort counsel has a habit of cross-examining experts by juggling bullets, by introducing other weapons and generally confusing the issues."

"Do you mean that I substitute evidence?" Mason asked angrily.

"I mean that you juggle evidence."

"That will do," Judge Kent ruled. "There will be no repartee between counsel. The Court will do the talking. The objection is overruled. The question will stand and the expert will be asked to make tests on the cartridge case presented to him by Mr. Perry Mason as counsel for the defense.

"And since the matter has come up, the Court will take this opportunity of stating that this is a perfectly legitimate question, regardless of where this cartridge case came from. This is an attempt to cross-examine the witness by testing his qualifications as an expert. If the witness has stated that one cartridge case came from a given weapon, it is certainly within the province of the defense to give him another cartridge case and ask him if that cartridge case also came from that same weapon.

"The Court is inclined to agree with Mr. Mason that in a case involving the life or liberty of a citizen, counsel representing the defendant should have the greatest latitude in cross-examination and that it is not the purpose or intent of the law to have the cross-examination confined to a conventional type of attack. If counsel has the ingenuity and the wit to bring in a collateral line of attack,

153

which is still pertinent but somewhat unconventional, counsel should be accorded that privilege.

"The Court may further state that the Court has heard criticism of Perry Mason's somewhat unorthodox methods of cross-examination before. That criticism is usually voiced by prosecutors.

"As far as this Court is concerned, the primary function of cross-examination is to test the recollection, the skill and the accuracy of witnesses. Any method, regardless of how unconventional or dramatic that method may be, which tends to bring about the desired object is going to be perfectly permissible in this court. It is far better to resort to the unorthodox and the dramatic than it is to have an innocent defendant convicted of crime.

"Since there is no jury present and this is a proceeding addressed to the sound discretion of the Court, the Court is also going to state that the Court itself is very anxious to have this question cleared up. Why in the name of sense should any person use a weapon in order to commit a murder, then return that weapon to a position where it is certain to be found and connected with the defendant, but first go to all the bother of mutilating the barrel so that the weapon cannot be identified?"

"May I answer that question?" Marshall asked Judge Kent.

"I'd be glad to have you *try* to do so," Judge Kent said.

"The answer is simply this," Marshall said. "The defendant perhaps did not deliberately intend to commit premeditated murder. She went to meet Mervin Selkirk, she possessed herself of a weapon. We don't know what happened at that meeting; that is for the defendant to tell us if she chooses to take the stand. But she did press the trigger of that gun and released the bullet which killed Mervin Selkirk. Then she returned to the room where she had been sleeping and, because she didn't know that the identity of the weapon could be checked by microscopic comparison of the impression made by the firing pin on the rim of the cartridge, she thought she would cover her back trail by mutilating the barrel of the weapon so that the weapon which fired the fatal bullet could never be identified."

"And then left the weapon under her pillow?" Judge Kent asked.

"Yes, Your Honor, we know she must have done that. The evidence shows she did."

Judge Kent shook his head indicating utter disbelief.

"The reason she did that," Marshall went on, "as we shall presently show, is that the weapon had been left on a table in the front hall. Under ordinary circumstances the weapon would have been returned to the bureau drawer in the front bedroom, which was the place it was usually kept. However that night the defendant was occupying the bedroom. So the gun was left in plain sight on the table.

"The defendant left her bedroom and tiptoed down the stairs. It is a fair inference that Mervin Selkirk either had an appointment with her or had found some way of communicating with her. She went downstairs, saw the gun, decided to take it with her, and fired one shot from it.

"Then when she returned to the house she had the gun with her. She went back to her room to decide what to do. She was worried for fear the fatal gun could be identified by ballistics experts so she roughed up the barrel."

"And then conveniently left it under her pillow?" Judge Kent asked skeptically.

"Yes, Your Honor, she was afraid she had left fingerprints on the gun and thought it would be better to say she had taken it from the hall table to her room. She didn't realize a ballistics expert could tell the barrel had been tampered with or that this tampering had been done after the last shell had been fired in the gun."

Judge Kent thought that over, then said dryly, "I take it that you have further evidence which you intend to introduce and which you hope and believe will support this position."

"We do."

"Very well," Judge Kent said, "the Court will keep an open mind. At the present time the Court is very frank to state that it considers the theory farfetched."

"The Court will bear in mind the imprint of the defendant's finger on the printing press which was found at the scene of the crime," Marshall said somewhat irritably.

"The Court will keep all of the evidence in mind," Judge Kent said, "and the Court will listen to you when you are ready to argue that evidence. I take it you are not ready to close your case and start the argument now?"

"No, Your Honor."

"Go ahead then and put on your other evidence," Judge Kent said. "In the meantime, the witness Redfield will be asked by the Court to check this cartridge case handed him by Mr. Mason.

"I take it, Mr. Mason, that you have some particular reason for making this suggestion, and that this particular cartridge case is of importance to your theory of the case?"

"It is, Your Honor."

"Very well. The witness Redfield will make that check and return to court with his report this afternoon," Judge Kent said.

Marshall said, "We'll call Miss Frances Delano to the stand."

Frances Delano, wearing the uniform of an airline hostess, came forward, was sworn and seated herself on the witness chair.

Judge Kent looked at the trim young woman approvingly.

Marshall said, "What is your occupation, Miss Delano?"

"I am employed as a stewardess on United Airlines."

"Where is your run?"

"Between San Francisco and Los Angeles, and Los Angeles and San Francisco."

"On the night of the seventeenth were you a stewardess

on a plane flying between San Francisco and Los Angeles?"

"I was."

"What was your schedule?"

"We left San Francisco at eight fifteen."

"I ask you to look at the defendant and ask you to tell us if you have ever seen her before."

"Yes, I have seen her. She was a passenger on my plane."

"There's no question about that," Perry Mason said. "That's stipulated, Your Honor. There's no need to call a witness to prove that."

"I am getting at something else," Marshall said.

He turned to the witness. "Now, Miss Delano, will you explain to us what happens with tickets which are purchased?"

"They're on a form," she said, "a folder. There are carbon copies made and at various control points the ticket part is torn off. There is a final carbon copy on the cover which is left in the possession of the passenger."

"I now show you a document and ask you if you can tell us what that is."

"May I see it?" Mason asked.

"Certainly," Marshall said.

He handed Mason a bloodstained, folded bit of heavy paper, then after Mason had inspected it, showed it to the witness.

The witness said, "That is the passenger's portion of a ticket. That is what the passenger retains on a one-way ticket."

"And this ticket has the name 'Miss N. Allison' on it?"

"That is correct."

"And what does that indicate?"

"That the ticket was issued to a Miss N. Allison."

"That is her signature?"

"No, that name was probably written by the person issuing the ticket. It is not necessarily the signature of the passenger, but this is retained by the passenger as an identification coupon and there's a memo so that in case of making out expense accounts or deductions for income tax purposes this is a voucher for the passenger."

"Cross-examine," Marshall said.

"No questions," Mason said.

"I would like to call Harry Nelson," Marshall said.

As Nelson was coming to the witness stand, Mason turned to Norda Allison. "That ticket has bloodstains on it," he whispered. "It must have been found on the body of Mervin Selkirk. Did you see him that night?"

"Absolutely not."

"How did he get possession of your ticket?"

"That," she said, "is more than I can tell you."

"Where was that ticket?" Mason asked, still whispering.

"In my purse."

Mason frowned. "If you're either lying or mistaken, you're going to get a jolt," he warned, then turned to face the witness stand.

Nelson was sworn, testified that he was a deputy coroner, that as such he had searched the clothes of the body of Mervin Selkirk when the body had been delivered at the morgue, that the airplane ticket identification cover which had been identified by the previous witness was in the inside right-hand pocket of the coat worn by Mervin Selkirk at the time the body was delivered to the morgue.

"Cross-examine," Marshall said.

"No questions," Mason said.

The bailiff approached Judge Kent on the bench and held a whispered conversation with him.

Mason took advantage of the opportunity to turn to Norda Allison.

"Was your purse ever out of your possession that night?"

"Not that I can remember."

Mason frowned. "You're going to have to account for that ticket," he whispered, "and you're going to have to tell a convincing story. Judge Kent has been with us all the way. He's ready to dismiss the case on the evidence so far introduced. He's not impressed by that gun having been found under your pillow. But this is something different."

Judge Kent looked up and said, "Gentlemen, I am going to ask the deputy district attorney and Mr. Mason to attend a conference in my chambers. A matter has come up in connection with this case which should be discussed in private. I can assure both counsel that the circumstances are very unusual. The Court will take its usual noon recess at this point and court is adjourned until two o'clock this afternoon. Will counsel please meet with me in my chambers?"

A policewoman approached to take Norda Allison into custody.

"You do some thinking about that ticket," Mason said. "There's something peculiar here, some explanation that . . . wait a minute! You had a suitcase with you?"

"Yes."

"That was checked?"

"Yes."

"Now then," Mason said, "the airplane companies sometimes staple the baggage check to the inside of the ticket stub. Was that done in your case?"

"Why . . . I guess so, yes."

"And when you arrived in Los Angeles, Lorraine Jennings and her husband met you?"

"Yes."

"Then," Mason said, "you would have surrendered your baggage check to Barton Jennings for him to get your suitcase."

"Not Barton Jennings," she said. "I think it was Lorraine. As I remember it, Barton went to get the car and Lorraine asked me for my baggage check. I think I tore off the baggage check and gave it to her and she . . . now wait a minute. She *may* have had the entire ticket stub."

"You think it over," Mason said. "That ticket stub got into the possession of Mervin Selkirk in some way. You're going to have to get on the stand and tell your story and you're going to have to tell exactly what happened."

"I . . . I just can't remember, Mr. Mason. It's my impression that I pulled the baggage check loose and left the stub of the ticket in my purse. I . . . I'm almost certain that's what happened."

"Now look," Mason said in an angry whisper, "don't be *almost* certain. If you just say you can't remember anything about it, I can probably convince Judge Kent that you handed the ticket stub to Barton Jennings so that he could claim your suitcase, and then we'll leave it up to Barton Jennings to explain what happened to the ticket; whether he dropped it, threw it away or put it in his pocket. But when you—"

"No," she said, with conviction. "The more I think of it, the more I'm *certain* that I tore the stub off and handed it to Lorraine Jennings. Her husband went to get the car while Lorraine took care of the suitcase. I know she was standing there with it and then Barton Jennings drove up in the car. A porter took my suitcase to the car and Jennings gave him a tip. I had put the ticket cover back in my purse."

"Well," Mason said, "think it over during the noon recess. I've got to go and see what Judge Kent wants. It's something rather important, otherwise he wouldn't have called a conference."

15

■

MASON PUSHED OPEN THE DOOR OF JUDGE KENT'S chambers and entered.

Manley Marshall was standing by the window. Judge Kent was seated at his big desk and seated to the right of the desk was Horace Livermore Selkirk.

Judge Kent said, "Come in, Mr. Mason. Sit down. You too, Mr. Marshall. A matter has been called to my attention which I think merits an off-the-record discussion."

Mason seated himself and after a moment Manley Marshall also seated himself.

Judge Kent looked at his watch. "I have telephoned the district attorney, Hamilton Burger, and asked him to attend this conference in person if he will. He should be here. He . . ."

The office door was pushed open and Hamilton Burger, somewhat short of breath, entered the judge's chambers. "How do you do, Judge Kent," he said.

"How do you do, Mr. Burger. Are you acquainted with Horace Livermore Selkirk?"

Selkirk got up and extended his hand. "Glad to meet you, Mr. Burger," he said.

"I have never met Mr. Selkirk personally," Burger said, beaming as he shook hands. "I have seen him at meetings and have heard him make a talk at a banquet, but have never met him personally. How do you do, Mr. Selkirk. It's indeed a very great pleasure."

"Sit down, gentlemen," Judge Kent said. "Mr. Selkirk has a communication of some importance in connection with a case which is pending before this Court. I felt, under the circumstances, the communication should be made in private, and I think that you gentlemen will agree with me it is not a matter for the press."

Burger nodded briefly to Perry Mason, seated himself, said, "Very well."

Horace Selkirk cleared his throat. "I am, of course, the father of Mervin Selkirk, the victim of the shooting in this case. I am the grandfather of Robert Selkirk, the seven-year-old son of Mervin Selkirk. Under the circumstances, Robert is the last of the Selkirk line. Mervin was my only child and Robert is his only child."

There was a moment of impressive silence.

"Under the circumstances," Horace Selkirk went on, "Robert is my sole heir.

"Robert's mother, who has been divorced and is now married to Barton Jennings, is in my opinion a shrewd, unscrupulous, scheming character. She knows that in all probability I will die before Robert attains his majority. She is not at all unaware of the fact that as Robert's legal guardian she would be entitled to certain perquisites and certain advantages, and, moreover, would be in a position to play upon Robert's sympathies and his natural affection for a mother so that she would eventually derive certain material advantages no matter how I tried to safeguard my estate—I can, of course, keep her from getting her fingers in most of my fortune, but Robert is impressionable and there is the bond of natural respect and affection."

Judge Kent frowned. "Does that have any bearing on the present case, Mr. Selkirk?" he asked. "I sympathize, of course, with your position. I know that you have lost a son under very tragic circumstances. I know that you must have undergone great emotional strain. But it would seem to me that the facts you have mentioned are somewhat extraneous."

"They are not extraneous," Horace Selkirk said coldly. "My grandson, Robert, killed his father, Mervin Selkirk."

"What?" Hamilton Burger all but shouted, half getting up from his chair.

Judge Kent leaned forward attentively frowning at Horace Selkirk.

"I know what I am talking about," Horace Selkirk said, "and Perry Mason also understands the situation. And Mr. Perry Mason intends to make a last-minute grandstand to save his client by showing what actually happened. I feel that in the interests of justice Mr. Mason should not be permitted to drag my grandson into the case and thereby place an irreparable stigma upon the boy's name."

"You say that Robert killed his father?" Judge Kent asked.

"Robert Selkirk was the instrumentality chosen by Lorraine Jennings to get rid of my son," Horace Selkirk said coldly. "Under a property settlement which had been made with my son at the time of the divorce, she received certain properties, and in the event of Mervin's death she not only received additional properties in her own name but Robert would inherit certain very valuable properties and she would naturally be the guardian of his person and estate, and as such entitled to compensation."

"I think," Hamilton Burger said, glancing suspiciously at Perry Mason, "we had better hear a little more about what you have in mind, Mr. Selkirk. And may I caution you not to be deceived by any elaborate scheme which may have been thought up by Perry Mason in order to extricate his client from a charge of first-degree murder. We have evidence in this case that points the finger directly at Norda Allison."

"Doubtless you do," Horace Selkirk said, "but that evidence has been carefully fabricated and you are the one who has been deceived, not me."

"You have some proof of your statements?" Judge Kent asked Selkirk.

"I have ample proof," Selkirk said.

"Perhaps you had better tell us what it is."

"I dislike to keep harping on this," Selkirk said, "but my son's ex-wife, Lorraine Jennings, is a very scheming, clever woman. She is, in my opinion, a fiend incarnate. She deliberately framed the seven-year-old Robert to be the innocent instrumentality of her hatred. I am not a demonstrative man, but I love my grandson very deeply.

"The child has been allowed to take an undue interest in firearms. He has been trained to watch television programs of the kind that are known as 'pistol pictures.' Then Lorraine permitted him to take the Colt Woodsman which has been introduced in evidence in this case and play with it, assuring him always that it was unloaded, but letting him point it and shoot it at people."

"You're certain of that?" Judge Kent interrupted incredulously.

"Evidence is available to that effect," Horace Selkirk said. "Neighbors who have watched proceedings at the Jennings house have seen the child pointing the pistol at people and pulling the trigger."

Judge Kent frowned.

"Then," Horace Selkirk went on, "after the boy had been properly conditioned to shoot this gun, believing it was always empty and unloaded, Lorraine Jennings let him have the weapon when it actually was loaded. Then she decoyed the child's father into going to the tent where the boy was sleeping, telling the father that he should surprise the boy. The thing happened which she hoped would happen. The boy heard the noise of the father entering the tent. He was wakened from a sound sleep. It was night. He had the gun with him, he raised it and pulled the trigger. The bullet entered my son's chest.

"My son staggered to his automobile in front of the house, leaving a bloody trail along the grass. He got in the car and drove away, trying to find help. He knew that a doctor, whom he felt could be trusted to treat his wound and say nothing, quite frequently played poker on Friday nights at the San Sebastian Country Club. He drove up there, not realizing the seriousness of his wound. He parked the car but before he was able to leave the car he became unconscious. Death ensued sometime after he became unconscious.

"I can produce proof of what I am talking about and I have reason to believe that Mr. Mason also has that proof. I am here to prevent the exploitation of my grandson."

"In what way?" Judge Kent asked.

"Perry Mason has been interrogating the neighbors," Selkirk said. "He has talked with some of them personally. He has talked with others by means of the private detective agency which handles his work in cases of this sort. He knows that a shot was fired from inside the tent where Robert was sleeping. He knows that shot inflicted a serious injury upon someone, that the person left a blood trail along the grass and that Barton Jennings arose early in the morning to eliminate this blood trail with a hose.

"Mr. Mason knows that my grandson was given the .22 Woodsman to play with, that the boy knew how to work the mechanism of the gun so as to pull back the barrel in a way that would cock it; then he would point the gun and pull the trigger. Mr. Mason has made careful inquiry and has all of this data at his finger tips.

"At the proper time, probably after court convenes this afternoon, he plans to ask Barton Jennings on cross-examination if it isn't a fact that the boy was permitted to play with this gun. He then intends to show that the boy had the gun on this fateful Friday night; that there was a trail of blood leading along the grass to the curb. Then Mr. Mason intends to ask the Court for an order bringing my grandson into court so that he can be interrogated.

"I wish to spare my grandson this frightful ordeal. It is true he is a bright little chap. It is true that he senses that something awful may have happened. He is not certain that he actually shot anyone, but he knows that he pulled the trigger of the gun and that the gun was loaded. He knows that it was pointed at some person who was about to enter his tent.

"Barton Jennings tried to convince my grandson that all

this was a horrible dream. a nightmare. I don't think he was able to convince the boy, but the boy certainly has no inkling at the present time that he actually killed his father. Nor does he have any idea that the killing of his father was part of a cold-blooded, deliberate plan hatched in the mind of the boy's mother.

"Mr. Mason is representing Norda Allison. As an attorney it is, I presume, his duty to do everything in his power to see that she is acquitted. However, Mr. Mason is well-known for his flair for the dramatic. He is looking for an opportunity to cross-examine Barton Jennings on the stand in such a way that the facts will be brought out in the most dramatic manner possible.

"When Mason has finished cross-examining Barton Jennings, Barton Jennings will be reduced to a hopeless wreck. The case will be so dramatized that Perry Mason will once more emerge as the invincible champion of the courtroom, and my grandson will have been stigmatized for life."

Horace Selkirk paused to survey Mason coldly.

Hamilton Burger, the district attorney, took a cigar from his pocket, clipped off the end and lit the cigar.

Judge Kent looked speculatively at Hamilton Burger's face. Then he looked at Mason, then back to Horace Selkirk.

"You are making rather sweeping charges, Mr. Selkirk," he said.

"I know what I'm talking about."

"You have proof?"

"Yes."

"What?"

Selkirk said, "I can produce my grandson, Robert, here in chambers within thirty minutes. I ask only that you, Judge Kent, take this young man into a private conference, where you—as a judge who is accustomed to handling problems with juveniles—can talk with him in a confidential manner. I suggest that you get his story. When you have that story, you will realize the truth of what I am saying."

Judge Kent frowned. "This procedure is, of course, highly irregular," he said. "As the judge in this case I am supposed to keep myself completely aloof from any outside influence."

"I grant you that," Selkirk said, "but as a citizen—a citizen who is not without some influence in the community, I may state—I feel that your primary function is to administer justice. I feel that it is going to be inhuman to allow Mr. Perry Mason to appear again in public as a master of legal legerdemain at the cost of wrecking the life of a seven-year-old boy. After all, Judge Kent, you are charged with looking after the rights of juveniles who, because of their tender age, must be, in a measure, wards of the state."

Again Judge Kent looked at Hamilton Burger.

Hamilton Burger removed the cigar from his mouth, blew out a wisp of pale blue smoke. His expression indicated that he was savoring the aroma of the cigar.

Manley Marshall sat there perfectly still, trying to look utterly noncommittal.

Judge Kent seemed somewhat irritated at Burger's attitude. "Do you," he asked, "know anything about this, Mr. Burger?"

Burger studied the tip of the cigar for a moment, holding the cigar between the thick first and second fingers of his powerful right hand. Then he said thoughtfully, "I'm not prepared to say that I know *nothing* about it. I am prepared to state that we consider this entire procedure irregular, that we wish to try our case in the courtroom, and particularly that I don't intend to disclose our evidence in this case in front of counsel for the defense. I simply don't intend to give him that advantage."

Judge Kent turned to Mason. "You have heard what Mr. Selkirk has said, Mr. Mason."

"I have heard what he has said."

"May I ask if there is some element of truth in it?"

"Since you ask, I can tell you that there is *some* element of truth in it. I'd like to ask Mr. Selkirk a question."

Mason turned to Horace Selkirk. "You are, I believe, attached to your grandson, Mr. Selkirk?"

Selkirk's face softened for a moment, then became hard. "That boy," he said, "is the only Selkirk who can carry on a proud name and the proud traditions of a proud family. I am proud of those traditions. I love him and I don't intend to see his life ruined."

"And," Mason said, "you would like to have his sole custody and guardianship?"

"That is beside the point."

"I don't think so," Mason said. "I would like to have you answer that question."

"You have no right to sit here and cross-examine me," Selkirk flared. "You know that I called the turn on you. You know exactly what you plan to do in connection with this case. You know the type of dramatic disclosure you intend to make when court reconvenes this afternoon. You know how you intend to cross-examine Barton Jennings. You know that you have been out getting information about the blood trail and about the gun."

"Do *you* know anything about a blood trail?" Judge Kent asked Hamilton Burger abruptly.

"Frankly, Your Honor, we do," Hamilton Burger said. "And, equally frankly, we don't think either Perry Mason or Mr. Selkirk knows *all* of the facts in this case. We are quite content to try this case in the courtroom, which is where it should be tried."

Judge Kent drummed on the desk with his fingers, then looked at Perry Mason. "Is it true that Robert Selkirk was permitted to play with a weapon, Mr. Mason?"

"I think it is," Mason said.

"The same weapon that has been introduced in evidence in this case as the murder gun?"

"I believe so, Your Honor. But that doesn't necessarily indicate it is the murder gun."

"I think it is the murder weapon," Hamilton Burger

said. "I think we've established that point by the imprint of the firing pin."

"I am not prepared to admit it," Mason said.

"Have you evidence concerning a blood trail, Mr. Mason?" Judge Kent asked.

"One of the neighbors has told me about it," Mason said.

"A *blood* trail, Mr. Mason?"

"That is my understanding," Mason said.

Judge Kent glanced across to Hamilton Burger. "I think the Court is entitled to find out more about this, Mr. District Attorney."

"Perhaps the Court is," Hamilton Burger said, "but counsel for the defense isn't."

"Just what do you mean by that?"

"I mean that there is no chance on earth that Robert Selkirk killed his father. The death of Mervin Selkirk was at the hands of Norda Allison. We are prepared to prove that."

"I take it you have a surprise witness?"

"A surprise witness, and we intend to keep this witness as a surprise witness."

Judge Kent thought for a moment, then turned to Horace Selkirk. "You have talked with your grandson?"

"Naturally."

"And you are sincere in your belief that your seven-year-old grandson, Robert, killed his father?"

"I feel absolutely certain of it."

"All right," Judge Kent said. "You get your grandson here without letting him know what it's all about. I'm going to talk with him during the noon recess. The procedure may be irregular, but I certainly am not going to let this case get to a point where it is made to appear in court that a seven-year-old boy inadvertently killed his father until I know more about the facts in the case.

"It may be that before I finish I will ask counsel to make certain stipulations, but in the meantime I am going to talk with this boy. How long will it take to get him here?"

"Fifteen minutes," Horace Selkirk said. "That is, if I may use your phone."

"Use the phone," Judge Kent snapped.

Selkirk crossed over to the phone, picked it up and asked for an outside line. Then he dialed a number.

Manley Marshall leaned over to whisper to Hamilton Burger, but Burger, holding up his left hand, gestured his assistant to silence.

The big district attorney puffed contentedly on his cigar.

Selkirk spoke into the telephone. "This is Horace Selkirk," he said. "How about the woman and the boy whom you were shadowing. Are they in the next room? All right," Selkirk said, "bring them up to the courthouse, to the chambers of Judge Homer F. Kent. Bring them up right away . . . I said bring them . . . All right, if they don't want to come we'll send an officer, but I don't want to waste that time. I want them here in fifteen minutes. Tell them that the judge has sent for them."

"Now, just a minute," Judge Kent said. "I didn't issue any such peremptory summons. I—"

"It's all right, Judge," Horace Selkirk said. "They'll be here. This woman is in my employ and she is supposed to do what I tell her to. I am the one who issues instructions."

Judge Kent looked at his watch. "Do you think they'll be here in fifteen minutes?"

"They certainly should be."

"That's cutting it rather thin," Judge Kent said. "I'm going to terminate this conference at this time. I am going to go to the lunch counter here in the building and get a quick sandwich. I will be back here in exactly twenty minutes—well, let us say twenty-five minutes. I will expect you gentlemen to meet me here, and when young Robert Selkirk comes in, I am going to suggest that I handle the interrogation of the young man. I don't want any interruptions. I don't want any suggestions from anyone. I am going to ask a few questions and, as you can readily understand, I don't intend to have the young man understand the object of those questions. I want to find out what actually happened and what he knows."

"You will understand," Selkirk said, "that I have so conditioned his mind that he actually knows only that he fired the gun. He doesn't know the person who ultimately received the bullet from that gun."

"I'll talk with him myself," Judge Kent said. "And since we are working on a very close time schedule, I will suggest that we terminate this conference at once and that we meet here in exactly twenty-five minutes. Is that satisfactory, gentlemen?"

Burger nodded.

"Quite satisfactory," Horace Selkirk said.

"I'll be here," Mason observed.

16

AT EXACTLY TWENTY-FIVE MINUTES AFTER JUDGE KENT had adjourned the meeting, the parties regrouped in the judge's chambers.

Judge Kent, who had evidently given the matter a great deal of serious thought during the intermission, regarded Horace Selkirk thoughtfully. "You are prepared to go ahead, Mr. Selkirk?" he asked.

"I am."

"My bailiff tells me that the woman and the boy whom you summoned are waiting in the witness room. They asked that word be sent to you."

"Very well."

"Do you wish to go and get them?"

"You can have the bailiff bring them in," Selkirk said. "I believe you said you wanted to be the one to examine the boy, and I don't want you to feel that I have been talking with him or telling him what to say."

"Very well," Judge Kent said. "The couple will be brought in. I am going to ask that you gentlemen remain quiet and let me ask the questions. I don't want any prompting, any suggestions or any instructions. Regardless of what the facts may show, this is a serious situation and a particularly serious situation in the life of a young man."

Judge Kent plugged in the intercommunicating speaker and said to his bailiff, "You may bring the woman and the boy in now."

There was a moment of tense, strained silence, then the door opened. A tall blonde woman and a seven-year-old boy entered the room; the boy looked a little dazed, the woman completely self-possessed.

"Come in," Judge Kent invited, "and sit down. Now, as I understand it, you're—"

Horace Selkirk's chair crashed over backwards as he jumped to his feet. *"Those* aren't the ones!" he shouted.

Judge Kent looked at him with annoyance. "It was understood that I—"

"Those aren't the ones! That isn't Robert! That isn't the woman! That—who the hell are *you?"* Selkirk shouted at the woman.

"That will do," Judge Kent rebuked. "We'll have no profanity here and no browbeating of this woman. May I ask who are you, madam?"

"I'm a detective," she said to Judge Kent. "I'm employed by the Drake Detective Agency. I have been instructed to occupy rooms 619 and 621 at the Anandale Hotel. I have done so."

"Who gave you those instructions!" Horace Selkirk shouted.

"Paul Drake."

There was a tense silence which was broken by Hamilton Burger's chuckle.

"This is no laughing matter, Mr. District Attorney," Judge Kent rebuked.

"I beg your pardon," Burger said, in a voice which showed no regret. "It is amusing to me to see someone else experiencing annoyance at the unconventional tactics of a certain well-known defense attorney."

"What became of Grace Hallum and Robert Selkirk who were in those rooms?" Horace Selkirk demanded.

"I'm sure I don't know," the woman said calmly. "I am a licensed detective. I act within the law. I followed the instructions of Paul Drake. I was told to go to the Anandale Hotel, to take my seven-year-old son with me and to remain there until I received further instructions.

"A short time ago I was advised that Judge Homer F. Kent had instructed me to leave the hotel and come here to his chambers. I promptly called Paul Drake for instructions and was advised by him to go to Judge Kent's chambers, take my son with me and give him my true name."

Horace Selkirk, his face livid, turned to Perry Mason. "This is once you can't get away with it!" he shouted. "I don't know what you've done with my grandson and the woman who has his custody, but this time you've really violated the law. You're guilty of kidnaping, at least technically."

Hamilton Burger surveyed Selkirk with speculative eyes. "Do you wish to charge Mason with kidnaping?" he asked. "If you do, and are willing to sign a complaint, we'll see that one is issued."

Horace Selkirk said with cold fury, "You're damn right I'll sign a complaint."

Judge Kent said dryly, "I once more want to caution you against profanity in these chambers, Mr. Selkirk, particularly in the presence of a child—now it is rapidly becoming apparent that this is a situation which should never have developed in this case. I feel that an attempt has been made to prejudice me by appealing to my sympathies and my desires to save a seven-year-old boy from an emotional shock. This inquiry has now gone far afield and if we are not careful I am going to be disqualified from continuing with this case."

Hamilton Burger got to his feet. "I think that is a point which could well have been made earlier in the case. I'm going to ask this woman and the boy to come with me. My office wants to ask some questions about what happened here, and if Mr. Selkirk wishes to take the responsibility of signing a complaint charging Mr. Perry Mason with kidnaping, I can assure him that the personal element in the situation will make no difference to my office. We will proceed without fear or favor."

Burger nodded to Selkirk and started for the door. "You come with me," he said to the woman detective.

Mason got to his feet, bowed to Judge Kent. "I'm sorry these matters had to interfere with your lunch hour," he said.

Judge Kent regarded Perry Mason with puzzled eyes. There was a faint hint of admiration back of his bewilderment.

17

COURT RECONVENED PROMPTLY AT TWO O'CLOCK. HAMilton Burger now sat in the prosecutor's chair alongside Manley Marshall.

"If the Court please," Hamilton Burger said, "I am going to call a witness who will eliminate any doubt in this matter. Call Millicent Bailey."

A woman in her late twenties came walking down the aisle. She was slender-waisted but well curved, and the rhythm of her walk showed that she was fully conscious of those curves. There was an almost defiant air about her as she entered the railed enclosure, held up her hand and took the oath.

She seated herself on the witness stand.

Hamilton Burger himself conducted the examination.

"Your name is Millicent Bailey?"

"Yes, sir."

"Miss or Mrs.?"

"Mrs."

"Are you living with your husband?"

"I am not. I'm divorced."

"I am going to call your attention to the night of the seventeenth and eighteenth of this month. Do you remember the occasion?"

"You mean the night of the seventeenth and the early morning of the eighteenth?"

"That's right."

"Yes, I remember them."

"May I ask what you were doing?"

"I was out with a boy friend."

"Do you wish to give us the name of that boy friend?"

"I do not. He is a respectable married man, but his home life is not happy. He is contemplating leaving his wife and filing an action for divorce, but I don't want anything that I may say to jeopardize his interests, and so I am not going to give his name."

"I feel certain," Hamilton Burger said, "that under the circumstances counsel will not press you for his name, and I know that I will not. I think as men of the world we'll appreciate the situation."

And Hamilton Burger bowed with elaborate courtesy to Perry Mason.

"I will not agree to restrict my cross-examination in the least," Mason said. "I will ask any questions that I feel are necessary to protect the interests of my client."

"Quite naturally," Hamilton Burger said, "but I feel that since it will soon develop that the identity of this man has absolutely nothing to do with the testimony of this witness, you will realize the expediency of refraining from bringing out the man's name."

Hamilton Burger turned back to the witness. "Now, Mrs. Bailey, I am going to ask you to describe generally what happened on the night of the seventeenth."

"I got off at eight o'clock. I went to my apartment and bathed and changed my clothes. My boy friend had said that he would call for me at ten o'clock.

"At ten o'clock he was there. We had a drink in my apartment and then we went to a night club where we danced until—well, it was somewhere around one o'clock."

"Then what happened?"

"Then we left the night club and took a drive."

"And where did you go on this drive?" Hamilton Burger asked.

"To the San Sebastian Country Club."

"Just where at the country club?" Burger asked.

"To the wide parking place where cars are parked; that is, a place which is reserved for the cars of members."

"What time was this?" Hamilton Burger asked.

"I can't tell you the time. It was perhaps one-thirty."

"That would be one-thirty in the morning of the eighteenth?"

"Yes."

"Just why did you go there?"

"We wanted to . . . to talk."

"Can you describe this parking place where you went?"

"Yes. There is a road which winds up the hill to the country club, then there is a very wide parking space where members can leave their cars. It is a big, flat space with lines ruled in it in white."

"When you drove up were there any other cars there?"

"Yes."

"I wish you would tell us exactly what happened after you arrived at the parking place," Hamilton Burger said.

"Well, there was a car there."

"Can you describe the car?"

"I didn't pay too much attention to it. It was a big car, one of the expensive cars."

"Were the lights on or off?"

"You mean on that car?"

"Yes."

"The lights were off."

"What was the car doing?"

"It was just sitting there."

"Did you see anybody in it?"

"No. I assumed the car had been left—"

"Never mind what you assumed," Hamilton Burger interrupted. "I am asking you only what you saw and what you heard."

"Yes, sir."

"What did you do?"

"My friend and I wanted to talk where we would be private. We . . . I mean, he, drove on past this car that was parked and went down to the car end of the parking lot. There are some trees there; some big live oaks, and there are perhaps half a dozen parking places that are right under these trees."

"And what did you do?"

"My friend parked his car there."

"Was the area lighted?"

"No, sir. There is a light, sort of a floodlight over the lawn in front of the entrance to the clubhouse that's on all night. There's a certain light from that which illuminates the parking place, but the parking place itself isn't really lighted up. It's fairly dark there."

"And *quite* dark under the trees?"

"Yes."

"Now, did your companion park the car so that it was facing into the trees?"

"No, sir, he did not. He turned the car around so that when we wanted to start out he only needed to step on the starter and pull right out."

"So you could see through the windshield and see the parking space?"

"Yes."

"And the road leading into the parking space?"

"Yes."

"And the car which was already parked there in the space?"

"Yes."

"Then what happened?"

"Well, we sat and talked."

"For how long?"

"For some time. We were trying to get things settled. I wasn't going to break up any home. I told him—"

"Now never mind what you talked about," Hamilton Burger said. "I am not going to interrogate you as to that point. I am simply trying to get the time element."

"Yes, sir."

"Do you know how long you were there?"

"Some little time."

"An hour?"

"I guess all of an hour."

"And what happened?"

"Well, we talked, and—"

"I'm not interested in that," Hamilton Burger said. "I want to find out . . . I'll get at it another way. What time did you leave there?"

"It was about . . . I guess about, well, perhaps half-past three in the morning; perhaps three o'clock, I don't know. I didn't look at my watch."

"Now, did anything happen just prior to the time you left?"

"Yes."

"What?"

"Another car came up the roadway to the parking place."

"That's what I'm trying to get at," Burger said. "Now, can you describe that car?"

"Yes, sir. It was an Oldsmobile and it had white side-wall tires."

"Do you know the license number?"

"I do."

"What was the license number?"

"JYJ 113."

"What did that car do?"

"It parked just behind this car that had been there all the time."

"Do you mean it went into a parking space alongside this parked car?"

"No, sir. It came to a stop right behind it. It wasn't in any parking place. It was right behind the car."

"And what happened?"

"Well, a woman got out of the car."

"You saw this woman?"

"Yes."

"Were the lights on?"

"In what car?"

"In the car that had just driven up."

"Yes, the lights were left on."

"You say that a woman got out?"

"Yes, sir."

"Do you know whether she was alone in the car?"

"There was no other person in the car."

"How could you tell?"

"When she got out, she left the door open and a light came on in the inside of the car—you know, the way a light automatically comes on when the door is left standing open."

"And what did this woman do?"

"She walked over to the parked car."

"Now then," Hamilton Burger said, "I'm going to show you a photograph of a car parked in the parking place at the San Sebastian Country Club and ask you if you recognize that car from the photograph."

"I do."

"What is it?"

"That is the car that was parked there that night."

"You mean the evening of the seventeenth and the early morning hours of the eighteenth?"

"Yes."

"The car which you have referred to as the car which was parked when you drove up?"

"Yes."

"The car which was there all the time you were parked under the trees there?"

"Yes."

"The car which was in front of the car that was driven by the woman?"

"Yes."

"Very well. Now, referring to the car which came driving up there, what did you do? What did you see?"

"I saw this woman get out of the car."

"And what, if anything, did she do?"

"She walked across to the parked car."

"And then what?"

"She paused by the door of that car. She took something from her purse."

"Could you tell what she took from her purse?"

"I think it was a gun."

"Did you see a gun?"

"I saw the light reflect from something metallic."

"And then what?"

"I don't know what happened after that. We got out of there, fast."

"Her car was still there when you drove out?"

"Yes."

"She was standing there?"

"Yes."

"Do you know whether she had seen your car; or that is, the car in which you were riding before you started the motor and turned on the lights?"

"I don't think she had. If she did, she hadn't paid any attention to it. It was when we drove out that she jerked back to look at us and I think she screamed; at least her mouth was wide open and I think she was screaming."

"Did you see her face?"

"I saw her face."

"Plainly?"

"Plainly."

"Would you recognize that woman if you saw her again?"

"I would."

"Do you see that woman here in court at this time?"

"I do."

"Can you point her out?"

The witness arose from the stand, leveled a pointing finger at Norda Allison and said, "That's the woman, the one sitting right there."

"The one sitting over here next to Mr. Perry Mason?"

"That's the one."

"Would you please step down from the witness stand and put your hand on her shoulder."

The witness marched down, placed her hand on Norda Allison's shoulder, turned and walked back to the witness stand.

Hamilton Burger smiled. "You may cross-examine," he said to Perry Mason.

Mason arose to face the witness. "When you entered the parking lot," he said, "were you sitting on the side nearest the parked car?"

"Yes."

"Then the car was parked on the right-hand side of the parking lot as you drove in?"

"Yes."

"Then as you drove out, the car would have been to your left?"

"Yes."

"Then you must have looked across the driver of the car; that is, the driver of the car in which you were riding, to see the two cars as you left?"

"What do you mean, the driver of the car?"

"Exactly what I said," Mason replied. "The driver of the car in which you were riding."

"I was driving the car."

"When you went out?"

"Yes."

"Where was your companion?" Mason asked.

"Crouched down on the floor in the back of the car," she announced defiantly.

There was a slight ripple of mirth in the courtroom which Judge Kent frowned into silence.

"Perhaps you can explain exactly what happened a little more clearly," Mason said.

"I've told you my boy friend was married. When we saw this car drive in there, the first thing we thought of was that it was one of those things—you know, a private-detective raiding party with a camera and flashbulbs. We thought his wife had framed him so as to get the kind of a settlement she wanted."

"Do you mean that she had framed him or caught him?"

"Well, caught him."

"That's what you both thought?"

"Sure," she said. "What else would you expect? This car comes driving up there around three o'clock in the morning, coming like sixty."

"Now, when you say one of those things," Mason asked, "do I gather that this is something usual in your life, that you have been previously photographed by some raiding party led by an irate wife?"

The witness was silent for a moment.

"We object, if the Court please," Hamilton Burger said. "That's not the proper cross-examination. The question is asked only for the purpose of degrading the witness. It is prejudicial misconduct on the part of counsel."

Judge Kent said, "There was that in the answer of the witness which seemed to invite the question. However, under the circumstances, I think it makes little difference in this case. The situation speaks for itself. The Court will sustain the objection."

"Were you sitting at the steering wheel when this other car came up the driveway?" Mason asked.

"No, I was not."

"Did you get behind the steering wheel at your own suggestion?"

"My boy friend suggested I had better drive it out."

"I take it then that he didn't see the woman who got out of the car?"

"He didn't see anything. He was down on the floor just as flat as he could get, and I took that car out of there just as fast as I could snake it out."

"But you did notice the license number of the car which drove up?"

"Sure."

"Why?"

"I thought . . . well, he said, 'My God, that's my wife,' and . . . well, I looked the car over, looked at the license plate and it was an easy license plate to remember and I told him that it wasn't his wife's car."

"You know his wife's car?"

"Yes, I've seen it."

"When you and your friend drove into the San Sebastian Country Club parking place you turned the car around so that it was headed out?"

"Yes."

"And why was that?"

"So we could make a quick getaway if we had to without having anyone get the license number of the car. If the car had been left headed into the trees, then we'd have had to back and turn."

"And the idea was that if you saw headlights coming you'd get out of there fast."

"Yes."

"But when you saw headlights coming you didn't get out of there immediately. You waited until after the other car had come to a stop and a woman had got out."

"Well . . . yes."

"And you got in the driving seat and the man who was with you remained in the rear."

"I didn't say he remained in the rear."

"Well, you did say he was on the floor in the rear."

"Yes."

"And that is right, is it?"

"Yes."

"Now when you identified the defendant you pointed a finger and said that the woman you had seen was the defendant at whom you were pointing."

"That's right. That was the truth."

"And then you got up and went down and put a hand on her shoulder."

"Yes, sir."

"Now, that identification had been carefully rehearsed, hadn't it?"

"What do you mean?"

"You had been talking with the deputy district attorney, Manley Marshall, about how you were to make that identification and he told you, 'Now, when I ask you if you can see that woman in the courtroom you are to point at the defendant. Just point right straight at her and say, That's the woman, sitting right there.' Didn't he say that?"

"Well, he told me to point at her."

"And did he tell you to put some feeling in your voice?"

"No, sir. He did not."

"Did he tell you that he was going to ask you to get up and walk down and put your hand on her shoulder?"

"No, sir."

"Didn't anyone tell you to put some feeling in your voice and be dramatic and say, 'That's the woman, sitting right there,' or words to that effect?"

"Well . . . that wasn't what you asked me."

"What do you mean?"

"You asked me if Mr. Marshall had said that."

"Oh, it was someone else that told you that?"

"Well, someone else told me to put some feeling in my voice when I said it, to make it dramatic, was the way he expressed it."

"And who was that?"

"Mr. Hamilton Burger, the district attorney."

"And when was that?"

"Just before I went on the witness stand."

"And did you repeat the words after Mr. Burger, 'That's the woman, sitting right there?'"

"Well, I . . . he told me that's what I was to say, and I said it."

"And he told you to put more feeling in it, didn't he?"

"Yes."

"So then you tried it again, with more feeling."

"Yes."

"Once or twice?"

"Two or three times. I . . . well, it's hard to be dramatic when you're not accustomed to acting. I guess you're inclined to say things in just an ordinary tone of voice, but Mr. Burger told me this was the dramatic high light of the trial and that I had to be dramatic about it."

Mason smiled. "That," he said, "is all."

"No questions," Hamilton Burger said, his face flushed an angry red.

The witness left the stand.

"I will now call Barton Jennings to the stand," Hamilton Burger said.

Barton Jennings, still using his cane, came forward, took the oath, and settled back in the witness chair, his stiff leg out in front of him. His hands clasped the head of the cane.

Hamilton Burger examined the witness and brought out the story from the time he had met Norda Allison at the airport to the time they had gone home. He got the witness to tell about Norda Allison and Perry Mason coming to the house, of Norda Allison's claim that she had seen the printing press in the storeroom. He had Barton Jennings identify the gun, and the witness testified that it was usually kept in the drawer of a dresser in the guest bedroom which was occupied that night by Norda Allison.

"Cross-examine," Hamilton Burger said to Mason.

Mason arose to stand in front of the witness. "I'm going to ask a few questions, Mr. Jennings," he said. "The answers to some of these questions may prove to be embarrassing, but I want to clear up certain matters. Now, your wife had been married before?"

"That is right."

"She had been married to Mervin Selkirk, the decedent?"

"Yes, sir."

"And there was a child, the issue of said marriage, Robert Selkirk?"

"Yes, sir."

"Robert lived with you and your wife from time to time?"

"Yes, sir."

"You are attached to him? That is, I mean, you are both attached to him?"

"Yes, sir. He is a very fine boy."

"And do you know where he is now?"

"Objected to," Hamilton Burger said. "Not proper examination and incompetent and irrelevant and immaterial. The whereabouts of this young man have no bearing on the present case. I see no reason for turning loose a lot of newspaper reporters to embarrass this young man."

Judge Kent thought for a moment, then said, "At the present time I am going to sustain the objection."

"Robert Selkirk was staying with you the night of the seventeenth and the morning of the eighteenth?"

"Yes, sir."

"You drove him away early on the morning of the eighteenth?"

"I took him away. Yes, sir."

"Why?"

"He was going to a gathering of young people."

"But he didn't go?"

"No."

"Why?"

"The dramatic events of the day made it inadvisable for him to go."

"But you didn't know that Mervin Selkirk was dead until quite a bit later than that, did you?"

"Later than what?"

"Later than when you took Robert away from your house."

"No, sir, I didn't."

"The young people were to rendezvous at about eleven o'clock?"

"I thought they were supposed to be there at seven o'clock. I now understand they didn't leave until eleven. I misunderstood the time over the telephone. I asked the man who was arranging the party what time the boys were to leave and I understood him to say that they would leave at seven o'clock, but to be there an hour before that. Later on I realized he had said eleven o'clock but I had misunderstood him."

"What time was it when you took Robert away?"

"It was . . . quite early. I don't know. I didn't look at my watch."

"And where did you take him?"

"There again," Hamilton Burger said, "I object. I have carefully refrained from asking this witness questions about Robert Selkirk, and counsel has no right to cross-examine him on that subject. The question is not proper cross-examination. It is incompetent, irrelevant and immaterial."

"I think I will permit this question," Judge Kent said. "You may answer. Where did you take Robert?"

"To a friend."

"A friend of his or a friend of yours?" Mason asked.

"Both."

"Now why did you take him away that early in the morning?" Mason asked.

"Because I didn't want him to be disturbed."

"Why?"

"Because—well, frankly, Mr. Mason, an action was to be brought and the object of that action was to get the sole custody of Robert; that is, my wife wanted to have his sole custody. Miss Allison, the defendant in this case, was going to testify as a witness; at least we hoped she would. I didn't want Robert to know anything about what was being planned until after the plans had been made. I didn't want him to hear the discussion."

"So you got up early in the morning and took him away?"

"Yes, sir."

"And that's your best explanation?"

"Yes, sir."

"Did you know when you took Robert away that he claimed he had discharged a gun during the night?"

"Objected to," Hamilton Burger said, "as incompetent, irrelevant and immaterial, as calling for hearsay testimony, and as not proper cross-examination."

"In the present form of the question I will sustain the objection," Judge Kent said.

"Did you take him away," Mason said, "because he had claimed during the night that he had fired a shot?"

"Same objection," Hamilton Burger said.

Judge Kent shook his head. "The question in its present form is permissible."

"All right," Barton Jennings said defiantly. "That may have entered into it."

"When did you first know that he claimed he had fired a shot during the night?"

"Objected to, not proper cross-examination, incompetent, irrelevant and immaterial," Burger said.

Judge Kent stroked the angle of his jaw, ran his hand around the back of his neck, rubbed the palm back and forth a few times and looked at Mason. "Aside from the technical rules of evidence, Mr. Mason," he said, "you must realize that the Court and counsel have certain responsibilities. Your questions and the answers of the witness will doubtless be given some prominence in the press, and the Court feels that the examination of the witness along these lines should be restricted to the legal issues, regardless of the technical rules of evidence."

Mason, on his feet, waited deferentially for Judge Kent to finish speaking. Then he said, "I am fully aware of that, if the Court please. But I am representing a client who is charged with murder. I am going to protect her interests. I can assure the Court that I am not merely asking questions for the purpose of clouding the issues. I have a very definite objective which the Court will see within a short time."

"Very well," Judge Kent said. "I am going to overrule the objection. The witness may answer the question."

Hamilton Burger said, "If we go into any part of this, Your Honor, I want to go into *all* of it."

Judge Kent hesitated, then said, "I think the evidence is pertinent. Defense counsel has a duty to perform. I am going to let the witness answer the question."

Barton Jennings said, "I guess it was about midnight, something like that, that Robert came crying into the house. I understand he told his mother that he had had a bad dream and he had fired a shot."

"Did he say he had had a bad dream?"

"Well, from what he told her I know I felt it was a bad dream."

"He thought someone had been in the tent?"

"He said he thought someone had been in the tent, groping along the bed. He had been awake at the time and it seems that this gun had been under his pillow."

Judge Kent said to the witness, "Robert told this to his mother?"

"That's right," Jennings said. "I had had one of my spells with my knee and had taken codeine. I was asleep."

Judge Kent looked over at Hamilton Burger. "This would seem to be hearsay, Mr. Prosecutor."

Hamilton Burger said angrily, "I'm not going to object. That's what counsel was hoping for. He hoped he could get headlines in the press and then have me shut him off. That's what I meant when I said that if we went into this we were going into it *all* the way. Robert told his mother about shooting the gun that night. The next morning he told this witness the same story."

Judge Kent said, "In the one instance it is part of the *res gestae*. In the other it is hearsay."

"We have no objection," Hamilton Burger said. "Having gone this far, it is only fair to the boy himself to go the rest of the way."

Judge Kent frowned.

"What gun was under Robert's pillow?" Mason asked.

"The gun that has been introduced in evidence, the Colt Woodsman, the .22 automatic."

"And he had pulled the trigger?"

"He had a dream. He dreamt he was pretending to be asleep. He heard someone prowling around the outside of the tent, or thought he did, and then he dreamt that this person entered the tent and at the height of the nightmare he thought that he had discharged the weapon."

"You say that was a nightmare?"

"Yes, sir."

"How do you know it was a nightmare?"

"Because the weapon was unloaded. It was empty when it was given to Robert."

"Who gave it to him?"

"I did, but I desire to explain that answer."

"Go ahead," Judge Kent said, "explain it."

"I had found out very shortly before that date that one of the baby sitters who had been employed to sit with Robert had been letting him use or play with this empty gun. Robert had some imitation weapons, as most boys do. He liked to play cowboy, city marshal, and things of that sort. He had, however, discovered there was a genuine weapon in the house and had been determined to play with that. One time when the baby sitter was having a great deal of trouble with him, in order to quiet him and keep him from having a nervous tantrum, she let him play with this weapon.

"I hadn't found that out until shortly before the seventeenth."

"How did you find it out?"

"I usually left the gun loaded and in the bureau drawer of the front room. At intervals I would clean and oil it. On or shortly before the sixteenth I took the gun out to oil it. It was unloaded and there were no shells in the magazine clip. This bothered me. I asked my wife about it and then I asked Robert about it. It was then that I found out about Robert having had the gun."

"And how did you happen to let Robert take the weapon on the night of the seventeenth and eighteenth?"

"We had to go to the airport to meet the defendant in the case. We didn't expect to be gone but a very short time. My wife is too nervous to drive but she wanted to be the one to greet the defendant at the airport, so I drove her there. Robert was asleep in a tent out in the patio, or that is, he was *going* to sleep in a tent out in the patio. I had asked some neighbors to come in and stay with him for the hour and a half it would take us to make the round trip and pick up the defendant."

"And what happened?"

"At the last minute it was impossible for the neighbors to come in. They had some unexpected company. I telephoned the agency which usually supplies us with baby sitters and it was impossible for either of our regular baby sitters to come that night. They were both engaged. Robert doesn't like to be with a strange baby sitter. I explained the situation to him. I told him he would be perfectly safe out there in his tent in the patio, and he said that it would be quite all right to leave him, provided he could have this unloaded gun under his pillow. It gave him a sense of security.

"In view of the fact that I had found out that he had been playing with the weapon, I made certain the gun was unloaded and let him have it."

"You yourself made certain that the gun was unloaded?"

"I did, yes, sir."

"Now then," Mason said, "when did you next see the gun?"

"Robert brought it in to his mother after the nightmare."

"And did she try to quiet him?"

"She did."

"Did he return to bed?"

"Yes. After he had become fully awakened, he realized that he had probably had a nightmare and he wanted to go back into the tent and go to sleep. As he expressed it, he wanted to be a 'real scout.' "

"And he did that?"

"Yes."

"And the weapon?"

"My wife put it on the hall stand. I wakened an hour or so after Robert had gone back to the tent. My wife told me what had happened."

"Where was the gun?"

"On the hall table. My wife placed it there intending to take it to its regular place in the bedroom after Miss Allison had left the room. Miss Allison was sleeping there that night."

"Was the gun unloaded at *that* time?"

"Of course it was unloaded."

"Did you at any time tamper with the barrel? Did you run a rattail file or any other instrument through the barrel?"

"No, sir."

"Or an emery cloth?"

"No, sir."

"Did you tamper with the barrel in any way?"

"No, sir."

"Did it occur to you that Robert might have loaded and fired the gun, that Robert's shot must have hit something and that the bullet could have been shown to have been fired from that gun, and therefore you roughed up the barrel so as to protect Robert?"

The witness shifted his position, then said, "No, sir."

"Because if you had," Mason pointed out, "in view of the testimony of the ballistics expert that the barrel had been tampered with *after* the last bullet had gone through the barrel, it would prove that this defendant couldn't have fired the fatal shot—at least with that gun. Do you understand that, Mr. Jennings?"

"Yes, sir."

"And you are positive you yourself didn't rough up the barrel to protect Robert?"

"I did not."

"Did you load the weapon?"

"I didn't load it. When I gave the gun to Robert I unloaded it."

"How about the barrel? Do you know whether there was a shell in the barrel?"

"I told you, Mr. Mason, that I unloaded the gun. I was very careful to unload it."

"You mean by that, that you worked the mechanism so as to be sure there was no shell in the gun?"

"Yes, sir."

"Then how did it happen Robert was able to fire the gun?"

"The answer is obvious. He only dreamt he fired it."

"And where was the gun the next time you saw it?"

"Under the pillow of the bed which had been occupied by the defendant."

"You were up rather early the morning of the eighteenth?"

"Yes, sir. I thought I had to take Robert away from the house earlier than was necessary. I have explained the reason for that."

"Now about washing away the blood that was on the front lawn," Mason said. "What can you tell us about that?"

"That is objected to," Hamilton Burger said, "as incompetent, irrelevant and immaterial. It is not proper cross-examination. I didn't ask this witness a thing about his activities in regard to a blood trail or anything that was on the lawn."

"The Court will overrule the objection," Judge Kent said. "This is a very interesting development in the case and the Court wants to go into it. The Court is trying to do substantial justice here and the Court doesn't care about technicalities, particularly at this time and on a matter of this sort. Answer the question, Mr. Jennings."

"There was no blood trail," Jennings said.

"Didn't you get up early and hose the lawn?"

"I got up early. I took Robert to a friend. I came back and no one seemed to be up in the house so I took a hose and watered the lawn."

"Didn't you actually hold the hose down on the lawn, washing it?"

"I may have directed a stream a short distance in front of me."

"And weren't you washing away a trail of blood?"

"Very definitely not."

"You weren't trying to do that?"

"No, sir."

"Did you notice any reddish tinge to the water which floated across the sidewalk and under the gutter while you were watering the lawn?"

"No, sir."

"Notice any red stains of blood in the gutter?"

"No, sir."

"Or at the curb?"

"No, sir."

"Are you prepared to state there were no such stains?"

"I am prepared to state that I didn't notice them."

"I notice that you are using a cane," Mason said.

"Yes, sir. I have trouble with my right knee. At times it becomes very stiff."

"I take it you have consulted a physician?"

"Certainly."

"Can you give me the name of any physician you consulted recently?"

"I haven't been to a physician recently—not about this."

"If the Court please," Hamilton Burger said, "I think this examination is getting far, far afield. I see no possible connection between this physical infirmity and the issues in this case."

"I do," Mason said. "I'd like to have the question answered."

"What is the connection, Mr. Mason?" Judge Kent asked.

"The connection is simply this," Mason said. "Barton Jennings went to the tent where Robert was sleeping. He listened in the doorway of the tent. Robert was feigning sleep. This witness thought Robert was fully asleep. He tiptoed into the tent, intending to get the weapon out from under Robert's pillow. He didn't speak as he entered the tent. Robert was frightened, and in his terror, pointed the gun and pulled the trigger. There was one shell in the barrel. That shell penetrated Barton Jennings' leg. Barton Jennings hurried out of the tent and across the lawn to the curb. He left a trail of blood. Somewhere out on the curb, or perhaps in a car, he managed to bandage his leg and stop up the flow of blood. He has, I believe, been afraid to go to a doctor for fear that the doctor would be forced to report the gunshot wound. I have every reason to believe that the .22 bullet it still in his leg, embedded either in the knee or in the fleshy part of the leg. I believe that if that bullet is extracted and the ballistics experts check the striations, it will be readily apparent that that bullet was fired from the same weapon which killed Mervin Selkirk. That is the reason for my entire line of examination."

"Your Honor! Your Honor!" Hamilton Burger shouted, jumping to his feet, gesticulating angrily. "This is the plainest kind of grandstand! This is the same old rigmarole, the same four-flushing tactics which counsel has employed in so many cases. This is a story which is made up out of whole cloth, something that has absolutely no support anywhere in the evidence."

"If you're so certain of that," Mason said, "let the witness pull up his trouser leg and let's look at that knee of his. Let's let the Court see the nature of the injury."

Barton Jennings, on the stand, said quietly, "Take a look if you want to."

He pulled up his trouser leg.

Judge Kent leaned forward. "There's no sign of a bullet wound or any other wound in that leg, Mr. Mason. The knee is swollen but there is no sign of a wound."

Hamilton Burger threw back his head and laughed. Spectators echoed the district attorney's laughter.

Judge Kent, angered, shouted, "Order! Order or I'll clear the courtroom."

He turned to Perry Mason, who seemed as calmly serene as if nothing had happened. "Is that all, Mr. Mason?"

"No, Your Honor," Mason said.

He turned to the witness. "I believe you own a very large dog," Mason said. "A Great Dane."

"Yes, sir."

"That Dane was on the premises on the night of the seventeenth?"

"He was."

"What is his name?"

"Rover."

"Was he on the premises on the morning of the eighteenth?"

"No, sir, he was not."

"What happened to him?"

Barton Jennings shifted his position on the witness stand. "I have rather inquisitive neighbors. I wanted it to appear that I had taken Robert to this expedition on which he was to depart, and that he had taken Rover with him. They knew the boys were supposed to take their dogs with them.

"Since, however, I was actually taking Robert to the

apartment of this friend, I made other arrangements for the dog."

"What other arrangements?" Mason asked.

"I don't think I need to answer that question," Jennings said.

"If the Court please," Hamilton Burger said, "this is all going very far afield. I have asked this witness certain particular questions. Counsel has taken him down a long, weary, winding path on cross-examination; a path filled with detours and irrelevant excursions. Surely, what this witness did with his dog is not proper cross-examination and is not a part of the issues in this case. I have been very patient in letting *everything* about this mysterious shot which had been fired at night be introduced in evidence, because I thought defense counsel was going to claim the bullet had lodged in the knee of this witness. I wanted counsel to expose the folly of his own position.

"I was also aware, Your Honor, that it might be claimed the firing of that shot and evidence concerning it might be considered part of the *res gestae*.

"Evidence about this dog is, however, an entirely different matter. No one can claim that what a witness does with his dog is part of the *res gestae*."

"I think I will sustain that objection," Judge Kent said.

"Did you," Mason asked Jennings, "notice a pool of blood by the curb on the morning of the eighteenth?"

"I have told you I did not."

Mason said, "I show you a morning newspaper which indicates that it has been stained with a reddish liquid."

"Yes, sir."

"Now then," Mason said, "I will state to the Court and counsel that I expect to prove this liquid is a mixture of water and blood, and I now expect to be able to show by a precipitin test that this is dog blood. Now I am going to ask you if it isn't a fact that Robert actually did fire that weapon on the night of the seventeenth or the early morning of the eighteenth, if the bullet didn't hit your dog, Rover, and if Rover didn't lose large quantities of blood.

I am going to ask you if you hadn't left your car parked at the curb and if you didn't take the bleeding Rover to your car, wrap him in a blanket so the blood wouldn't get on the car, and drive him hurriedly to a veterinarian."

"The same objection," Hamilton Burger hastily interposed. "This is getting at the same matter in a slightly different form of questioning. The Court has already ruled on it."

"Well, the Court is going to reverse its ruling," Judge Kent said. "The question as it is now framed by counsel certainly indicates a situation which should be inquired into and which may well be pertinent to the issues in this case. The witness will answer the question."

Jennings gave every evidence of uneasiness. "I found my dog had been hurt," he said. "I took him to a veterinarian."

"What veterinarian?"

"I don't think I have to tell that."

"What veterinarian?" Mason asked.

"Dr. Canfield," Jennings said sullenly.

"At what time did you take him there?"

"About one o'clock in the morning, I guess."

"Now," Mason said, "let us assume for the sake of this question that young Robert woke up from a sound sleep, that he was startled, that he thought someone was about to attack him, that he had this weapon under his pillow and that the weapon, in some manner, had become loaded. He raised the weapon and pulled the trigger. He could very well have shot this dog, Rover, couldn't he?"

"I suppose he could have. I don't know. I found Rover bleeding. He evidently had been injured. I didn't know whether he'd been struck by an automobile or what had happened, so I took him to a veterinarian."

"And did the veterinarian work on the dog?"

"Yes, sir."

"Did the veterinarian tell you what was wrong with the dog?"

"I don't know. I didn't wait to find out. I left the dog, told the veterinarian to do whatever was required and then returned home."

"Have you seen the dog since?"

Again Jennings hesitated, then said, "Yes, the dog is recovering."

"From a bullet wound?"

"I have not asked."

"Have you been informed?"

"I told the veterinarian I didn't care about the details, all I wanted was for the dog to get well."

"If the Court please," Mason said, "an X ray can determine if a bullet is somewhere in the dog's body. If the bullet was fired from the same gun which killed Mervin Selkirk, the bullets will have the same characteristics. It can, therefore, be determined that the bullet which killed Mervin Selkirk was fired from the Jennings gun, despite the fact that the barrel has been mutilated so that it is impossible to get the characteristics of that barrel with a test bullet."

Jennings moistened his lips with the tip of his tongue. Hamilton Burger started to say something, then changed his mind.

"Now then," Mason went on, "Robert subsequently told you that a man had been entering the tent where he was sleeping?"

"Yes."

"That was supposed to have happened before you had taken the dog to the veterinarian?"

"Yes."

"And that dog was a trained watchdog?"

"Yes."

"He would have guarded Robert with his life?"

"Yes."

"But the dog made no noise?"

"No. That's how I knew it was just a dream that Robert had," Barton Jennings said triumphantly.

"Yes," Mason said, "it could have been a dream, or it

could have been that the man who was entering the tent was one that the dog trusted. Suppose Mervin Selkirk had gone to the tent to kidnap Robert, or suppose you yourself had decided you wanted that gun, Mr. Jennings. Suppose you went to the tent and listened. You heard Robert apparently sleeping peacefully so you tiptoed your way into the tent without speaking, hoping to reach under his pillow and get the gun, and then suddenly there was the roar of an explosion. You heard the bullet hit the body of the dog, the dog ran from the tent and you ran after him. You saw that the dog was bleeding quite badly. You had left your car with the license number JYJ 113 parked at the curb. You hurriedly wrapped a blanket around the dog and rushed him to the veterinarian. Then you returned to the house, parked your car in front of the house and entered to have your wife tell you about the story Robert had told of firing the gun."

"It didn't happen that way. I was asleep. I didn't hear about Robert's dream until much later."

"Tut-tut," Mason said. "A neighbor remembers hearing the sound of a shot. You admit that you took the dog to Dr. Canfield, the veterinarian. We will check Dr. Canfield's records and I think we will find that those records show you arrived at his place with the wounded dog prior to one o'clock in the morning."

"Well, what if I did?"

"Then you couldn't have been asleep while Robert was relating his dream," Mason said.

"All right," Barton Jennings said, "I wasn't asleep. I had taken the dog to the veterinarian just as you suggest."

"You were wakened by the shot?"

Jennings hesitated, then said, "Yes, I was wakened by the shot."

"And dressed?"

"Yes."

"And then went out to the tent to see what had caused the shot?"

"No, I went to the wounded dog."

"And where was the wounded dog?"

"Lying by the car."

Mason smiled and shook his head. "You're wrong, Jennings. The wounded dog wouldn't have gone to the car unless you had taken him to the car. The wounded dog would have gone to the house, looking for help. The fact that the dog went directly to the car and that there was a trail of blood on the lawn leading to the car indicates that you were with the dog at the time he was shot."

"That question is argumentative, if the Court please," Hamilton Burger said.

"It may be argumentative, but its logic is so forceful that the Court will take judicial cognizance of it," Judge Kent said.

He leaned forward. "Mr. Jennings."

"Yes, Your Honor."

"Look at me."

The witness turned to look at the Court.

"You have already contradicted yourself upon two or three vital points. Those contradictions when a person is under oath constitute perjury, and perjury is punishable by imprisonment. Now I want to know what happened. Did you take the dog to the car after the dog was shot?"

Jennings hesitated, looked down at his feet, looked at Hamilton Burger, then hastily avoided his eyes, turned to Perry Mason, found no comfort there, and remained silent with his eyes downcast.

"Did you?" Judge Kent asked.

"Yes," Barton Jennings said after a moment.

"In other words," Mason said, "you went out to the tent to get that gun from under Robert's pillow, didn't you?"

"Well . . . all right, I did."

"You listened at the tent and heard Robert breathing regularly and thought he was sleeping?"

201

"Yes."

"You didn't realize until afterward that Robert, not recognizing you and utterly terrified, was feigning sleep, but had the gun in his hand."

"I guess so, yes."

"So you entered the tent with the dog either at your heels or just in front of you. You reached out toward the pillow and it was then that Robert shot."

"All right."

"As you heard the bullet hit the dog, you turned and raced out of the tent and saw that the dog was injured. You remembered that your automobile was parked there at the curb and you raced toward the automobile with the dog following you.

"While you were getting the door of the automobile open, the dog stood there, and there was a pool of blood at the curb where he stood. Then you wrapped the dog in a blanket, got him in the automobile and hurried to the veterinarian. You left the dog and then returned as fast as you could to your home. You found your wife had comforted Robert and had put him back to bed. Your wife had told Robert that you were sleeping in the bedroom, but actually she knew better."

Jennings was silent.

"Is that what happened?" Mason asked.

"Yes," Jennings said, "that's what happened."

"So then," Mason said, "you took the gun which your wife had taken from Robert. What did you do with it?"

"My wife had put it on the hall stand. I picked it up and looked at it, then left it on the hall stand and went back to bed."

"And when you put it back on the hall stand, you must have loaded the magazine and put the clip of ammunition back in the gun."

"I guess I must have. I guess that's right."

"And then you went to bed?"

"Yes."

"And you believe that sometime during the night the

defendant got up, left her bedroom, went down to the hall stand, got the gun, went out to your car with license plate bearing the number JYJ 113 which you had left parked at the curb, drove out to the San Sebastian Country Club and killed Mervin Selkirk."

"She must have. There's no other explanation. The evidence shows she did."

"How did she know that Mervin Selkirk was to be at the San Sebastian Country Club?"

"I don't know."

"How did she know that your car was left at the curb with the key in it?"

"She saw me park the car there."

"And leave the key in it?"

"I don't know, I may have— No, wait a minute, I left the key in it when I returned from the veterinarian's office. I was excited."

"And who used a rattail file to roughen up the barrel of the gun so that the ballistics experts could not tell what gun had fired the fatal bullet?"

"I presume she did."

"Why?"

"So that the gun couldn't be traced to her."

"Then having done that, she deliberately left the gun under the pillow of the bed where she had been sleeping?"

"She probably did that inadvertently."

Mason smiled and shook his head. "The gun was registered in *your name*, Mr. Jennings. *You* were the one who would be more interested than anyone in making it impossible for the fatal bullet to be traced."

Jennings said nothing.

"And you now think that you must have loaded the gun after your wife put it on the hall stand?"

"Yes. I must have."

"Then where did you get the shells? You surely didn't go to the defendant's room?"

Jennings rubbed his cheek with a nervous hand. "I guess I was mistaken. I couldn't have loaded the gun."

"Then if the defendant fired the gun, she must have descended the stairs, found the gun, inspected it, found it was unloaded, then climbed the stairs to her room, found the box of shells, loaded the gun and then gone to the country club to kill Mervin Selkirk?"

"I . . . I guess that's right."

"How would she have known there was ammunition in the room?"

"She must have found it."

"How would she have known the gun was on the hall table?"

"She must have seen it when she started out."

"How would she have known it was unloaded?"

"She must have inspected it."

"And then climbed the stairs to her room to get shells?"

"Of course. Why don't you ask *her*?"

"I'm asking you."

"I don't know what she did."

"Now, when your dog was shot at perhaps twelve-thirty to one o'clock on the morning of the eighteenth, the barrel of the gun hadn't been tampered with, had it?"

"No."

"Then if the bullet is still in the dog, that bullet can be recovered by a surgical operation and the individual characteristics of the barrel of your gun can be determined just the same as though a test bullet had been fired from it. In other words, the bullet which was fired into the dog would then become a test bullet."

"I guess so."

"And how do you know that the barrel of the gun hadn't been tampered with at the time the dog was shot?"

"I . . . I don't know."

"Yes, you do," Mason said. "You know because you were the one who tampered with the barrel. You were the one who used the rattail file. You were the one who knew that Mervin Selkirk was to be at the San Sebastian Country Club and you went out there to kill him."

"I didn't do any such thing," Barton Jennings said, "and you can't prove it."

"Then," Mason asked smilingly, "why did you go out to Robert's tent at twelve-thirty-five on the morning of the eighteenth to get the gun which was under Robert's pillow?"

"Because I didn't think it was a good thing for the boy to sleep there with a gun."

"Then why didn't you get the gun before you had gone to bed?"

"I didn't think of it."

"You knew he had the gun?"

"Well, yes."

"But you didn't think of it until after you went to bed?"

"Well, it wasn't until after I went to bed that I . . . well, that's right, I got up and dressed and went out to get the gun."

"Did you waken your wife when you dressed?"

"No, she was sound asleep."

"But she wakened when she heard the shot?"

"I don't think so. She wakened when Robert came running into the house, telling the story of his nightmare."

"Of what you have characterized as his nightmare," Mason said. "Actually, Robert told exactly what had happened; that he. had wakened to find a man groping his way toward his bed, that he had instinctively thrown up the gun and pulled the trigger."

Barton Jennings was silent.

"I think," Mason said, "I have no further questions of this witness."

"I have no questions on redirect examination," Hamilton Burger said. "I may state to the Court that while this cross-examination has revealed many unexpected developments, the fact remains that the positive identification of the defendant speaks for itself."

"I'm not certain it does," Judge Kent said.

"I would like to ask a few more questions of Millicent Bailey on cross-examination," Mason said.

"Very well. Mrs. Bailey, you may return to the witness stand," Judge Kent ruled.

"Your Honor, I object," Hamilton Burger said. "This is a piecemeal cross-examination and—"

"And it is entirely within the control of the Court," Judge Kent ruled. "Recent developments have made the testimony of this witness appear in an entirely different light. Return to the stand, Mrs. Bailey. Mr. Mason, you may proceed with your cross-examination."

Mason said, "Mrs. Bailey, you state that you saw the defendant at around three or three-thirty on the morning of the eighteenth?"

"Yes, sir."

"When did you next see her?"

"On the morning of the nineteenth, at about ten o'clock."

"Where did you see her?"

"I picked her out of a line-up at police headquarters."

"How many other people were in that line-up?"

"There were five women in all."

"And you picked the defendant as being the one you had seen?"

"Yes."

"Now that was the next time you had seen the defendant?"

"Yes."

"You hadn't seen her after that time when you saw her in the morning at about three or three-thirty, or somewhere in there?"

"Well, I . . . I had had a glimpse of her."

"Oh, you had had a glimpse of her. Where was that?"

"At police headquarters."

"And where did you see her at police headquarters?"

"I saw her when she was being escorted into the show-up box."

"Was anyone with her at that time?"

"A police officer."

"Were there any other people in the showup box?"

"Not at that time, no."

"The defendant was put in there by herself?"

"Yes."

"And you had a good look at her?"

"Yes."

"And then afterwards four other women were brought into the showup box?"

"Yes."

"And then the officers asked you to pick out the one that you had seen out there at the San Sebastian Country Club?"

"Yes."

"And you unerringly picked the defendant?"

"Yes."

Mason said, "I am going to ask Mrs. Barton Jennings to please stand."

There was silence in the courtroom.

"Please stand, Mrs. Jennings," Mason said.

Lorraine Jennings made no move to get to her feet.

"Stand up, Mrs. Jennings," Judge Kent ordered.

Reluctantly Lorraine Jennings stood.

"Will you come forward, please?" Mason asked.

"Come forward," Judge Kent ruled.

"Now then," Mason said to Mrs. Bailey, "is there any chance that this is the person whom you saw getting out of the car and approaching the car that was parked at the San Sebastian Country Club?"

The witness studied Mrs. Jennings for a long moment, then said, "I . . . I don't think so."

"But it could have been?"

"Well, she's got very much the same build and complexion as the defendant, but I . . . no, I don't think so."

"That's all, Mrs. Jennings," Mason said.

Lorraine Jennings turned abruptly and walked so rapidly she was almost running.

"Wait! Wait!" the witness said.

"Wait, Mrs. Jennings," Mason said.

Mrs. Jennings paid no attention.

"Now that she walks rapidly," the witness said excitedly, "I know that it was this woman. There's a peculiar way she has when she walks; that hurrying walk, that was just the way she walked when we saw her."

Mason smiled and said to Hamilton Burger, "That, Mr. District Attorney, concludes my cross-examination. Do you have any redirect examination?"

Hamilton Burger slowly got to his feet. "If the Court please," he said wearily, "I suggest that this matter should be adjourned until tomorrow morning at ten o'clock. There are some things which I feel should be investigated."

"I think so, too," Judge Kent said dryly. "The case is adjourned until tomorrow morning at ten o'clock, and in the meantime this defendant is released on her own recognizance."

18

■

MASON AND DELLA STREET WERE IN THE LAWYER'S private office when Drake's code knock sounded on the door.

"Let Paul in," Mason said wearily.

Della Street opened the door.

Drake, grinning broadly, said, "Well you did it, Perry."

"What happened?" Mason asked.

"Complete confessions," Drake said. "Also, you have a suit against Horace Livermore Selkirk. He filed a complaint charging you with kidnaping, then it turned out you had sent the boy to the place where his mother told him to go, and Hamilton Burger's face is red over that."

"But what about the case itself? What about the murder?" Mason asked.

"Mervin Selkirk was a cold-blooded, highly efficient individual. I guess he took after his dad as far as his efficiency and ruthlessness were concerned," Drake said. "When Lorraine left him and married Barton Jennings, Selkirk quietly proceeded to get all the information he could on Barton Jennings. It was plenty. He found that Jennings was treasurer and manager of the Savings and Loan Corporation. Selkirk deliberately schemed to get Jennings to invest in some so-called sure things, and before Jennings knew it, he was hopelessly involved. Then Mervin Selkirk began to put on the pressure. He owned Barton Jennings, body and soul.

"Lorraine had no idea there was any contact between the two men, but her husband was reporting regularly to her ex-husband.

"When Lorraine got together with Norda Allison and wanted to get sole custody of Robert, Selkirk cracked the whip. He had previously forced Barton Jennings to get a printing press and print the envelopes which had been used to mail the threatening letters to Norda Allison. That press had been at Jennings' office, concealed in a closet, until the day before the murder. At that time Jennings' secretary had announced she was planning to clean out the closet and get rid of a lot of junk that had been accumulating over the years.

"So, while Lorraine Jennings was away that afternoon, Barton Jennings had taken the printing press and the envelopes to a temporary place of concealment in his basement. He had previously reported to Selkirk that Norda was going to join his wife in Los Angeles and that a move was to be made to get sole custody of Robert for Lorraine.

"Mervin Selkirk ordered Barton to listen in on their plan and then sneak out of the house to meet him at the San

Sebastian Country Club at one-thirty in the morning. He gave Barton an ultimatum. Either Barton was to fix things so that Lorraine gave up all claim to Robert, or Selkirk was going to expose Barton Jennings, have him sent to prison, and use that to defeat the application for custody of the child.

"That evening, on the way back from the airport, was when Jennings made up his mind to kill Selkirk but the only gun that he could put his hands on was under Robert's pillow. He went out to get the gun. Robert was panic-stricken and fired the gun. The bullet hit the dog.

"Jennings took the dog to the veterinarian, came back, found his wife had quieted Robert, and then confessed everything to his wife. He went out for a showdown with Mervin Selkirk. In the course of that showdown he shot Selkirk, probably just a few minutes before Millicent Bailey and her boy friend drove up. Then Jennings returned to the house. His wife was waiting up for him. He told her what had happened. Then he went down to his workshop to rough up the barrel of the gun.

"While he was doing that, Lorraine decided to frame the crime on Norda Allison. She still had Norda Allison's airplane ticket. She got in the car, went out to the place where the death car was parked and dipped Norda Allison's ticket into the pool of blood on the floor of the car, then put it in the side pocket of Selkirk's coat. She didn't realize that Millicent Bailey and her boy friend were doing a little necking and that they had seen her drive up. When Millicent drove out, Lorraine was in a panic. But she still went ahead with her plan to frame the crime on Norda Allison because that was the only thing left for her to do.

"When Barton Jennings had roughed up the barrel of the gun with a rattail file, Lorraine placed it under Norda's pillow after Norda had left. In their anxiety to make the case look good they overdid it.

"However, the police played right into their hands. Having come to the conclusion that Norda Allison was guilty, they virtually forced Millicent Bailey's identification.

"After they had planted the gun under the pillow, Barton Jennings suddenly remembered the printing press down in the spare room, the one he had used in printing the envelopes which he sent to Norda Allison in San Francisco.

"He had no way of knowing Norda had found this press. The only sleep Jennings and his wife got that night was after Jennings had moved Robert, washed the dog's blood from the grass and while they were waiting for Norda to get up. They were so tired they slept soundly for a couple of hours and didn't hear Norda in the basement.

"By that time Jennings felt it could be made to appear Mervin Selkirk had had the printing press in his car and that Selkirk had been printing the envelopes, just as Norda had suspected all along.

"So Jennings loaded the printing press in the trunk of his car and drove out to the country club to scout around. Selkirk's body hadn't been found as yet, but since it was broad daylight Jennings didn't dare park in the parking place. He did, however, explore the service road and find a place where his car was out of sight, both from the country club headquarters, as well as from the parking lot.

"He got rid of the press and returned home. By that time Lorraine had learned of Norda's departure. They realized, of course, she must have discovered something, so they became more determined than ever to frame the murder on her. They sat there, waiting for the explosion to take place. They were, however, frightened to death when Norda showed up with you. They had no way of knowing she'd found the printing press. That must have been a real jolt."

"He's confessed?" Mason asked.

"They've both confessed," Drake said.

"What about Norda Allison?" Mason asked.

"You don't need to ask that one," Drake said. "She was released on her own recognizance, you'll remember, and she and this Nathan Benedict did quite a bit of dining and dancing at The Purple Swan Night Club. They drove away in Benedict's rented car and somehow my operative, who was trying to tag along, got lost in the shuffle. That was about one-thirty. Norda Allison showed up in front of her hotel at three-forty-five this morning. She seemed to be walking on air. Nathan Benedict, who drove her to the hotel, escorted her in, and my man didn't have any trouble following him after that. He went directly to his hotel and went to bed."

"I see," Mason said dryly.

"So that's the case," Drake commented.

"Well, I'm sorry," Mason said. "I'm sorry for Robert . . . although, when you come right down to it, a jury isn't going to be too tough on Barton Jennings for killing a man who was blackmailing him. They'll make it manslaughter. I don't know but what a proper presentation of the case might get Lorraine Jennings out of it scot-free without a prison sentence. After all, a court will consider Mervin Selkirk's character if she applies for probation and . . ."

The phone rang.

Della Street picked up the instrument, said to the receptionist, "Hello, what is it, Gertie?"

"Just a minute," she said.

Della Street turned to Perry Mason. "Lorraine Jennings is calling you. Gertie says she's absolutely frantic. She wants to know if you'll go to the detention ward to see her."

Mason hesitated for a long five seconds, then slowly nodded. "Tell her that I'll be down to see her," he said. And then added, "For Robert's sake. I guess I owe them both that much, and I can use my claim against the grandfather for filing a false charge to make him go along. He really loves Robert, and I guess we can make him quit being quite such a cold-blooded greedy grandfather and get him to co-operate with Lorraine in doing whatever is best for Robert.

"Tell her I'll be down to see her, Della."

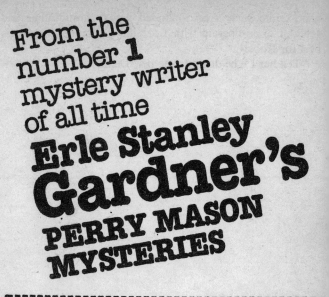